drama diaries

unfamous

by Lainey McBride

by Betsy Howie

Illustrated by Mike Lowery

D1258966

SCHOLASTIC INC.

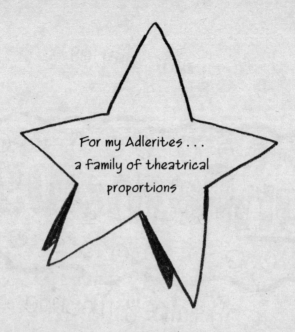

For my Adlerites . . .
a family of theatrical
proportions

ISBN 978-0-545-39707-0

Text copyright © 2013 by Betsy Howie
Cover art by Allison Cole.
Interior art by Mike Lowery.
All rights reserved. Published by Scholastic Inc.

12 11 10 9 8 7 6 5 4 3 2 1   13 14 15 16 17 18/0

Printed in the U.S.A.   40
First Scholastic printing, February 2013
Book design by Jennifer Rinaldi Windau

LLM&F

Dear Writer/Researcher/Fan,

Welcome to the world of Lainey McBride. As you probably know from reading the first volume of her Drama Diaries, this archive is a full accounting of the life of Lainey McBride. This is where every important thought, conversation, and keepsake that involves Lainey McBride is held. You could call it her own personal archive.

This volume has been put together by Lainey McBride herself. She began her archival work at the age of twelve as a courtesy to her future biographers and fans (you).

We hope you find these pages enlightening and fascinating. We sure did.

Sincerely,

The Legendary Lainey McBride Foundation

Greetings, fans, friends, and family! *Lainey McBride, PFP*, here. That's *Pre-Famous Person* for those of you who are new to my Drama Diaries. I am going to be extremely famous—hopefully in the near future, but if not, at some point—and therefore, it will be helpful for biographers to know that this was written before that happened. Thus, the *Pre*-Famous-Person clarification.

Okay. Moving on. There is a lot to tell you. It's been a couple of weeks since I've written. In all honesty, I needed some quiet time after the terrible moment when I did NOT get the role of Anne Frank in the production over in Kokomo. It would have been bad no matter what, but the fact that Rodney Vaccaro is directing the show makes it even worse. Because, as I told you in my first volume, Rodney Vaccaro is an incredibly important all-around essential Indiana showbiz connection. Working with him would have been extremely excellent for my career.

I've been trying to meditate in order to rise above this situation. That's what Maeve Winkley (the most EXTRAORDINARY performer who has ever lived!) does when she doesn't get a part. I read that in *People*. I'm not sure how it's supposed to help, but I'm trying it anyway. I sit cross-legged on the floor next to my bed, close my eyes, and hum. I Googled *meditation* and that's what popped up.

I'm not so sure it's working though, because every time I think

I've gotten over not being cast, somebody asks me whether I got the part! Or, there's a mention in the newspaper about the upcoming production starring NOT ME, or in the case of last night, I get an email from Libby Chamber—who IS starring in the production!

WHAAAAT?!

Libby Chamber. Hmmm. How to describe Libby Chamber . . . Well, let's see . . . hmmmm . . . I don't know . . . Oh, wait! I remember now.

SNAKE!!!!

Except she keeps acting like we're friends!

FROM: StarChamber@yippee.com
TO: LaLaLainey@yippee.com

SUBJECT: Movie! Movie! Movie!

Lainey!!!

I could hardly wait to get home from rehearsal because all I wanted to do was send you this email to tell you that A MOVIE IS GOING TO BE SHOT IN . . . (HOLD ON TO YOUR HAT!) . . . FAIRMOUNT!!!

Remember a few months ago when you and I both ran into Rodney at the Franklin Hotel? That's when he was showing a Hollywood location scout a bunch of different towns all over Indiana.

Well, Rodney announced at rehearsal tonight that they decided that Fairmount is the one! ISN'T THAT A-M-A-Z-I-N-G?!?!?!?

Let me just interrupt this email to say—WHAAAT?!—again. Why is she telling me this? Why is she giving me the inside scoop on this UNBELIEVABLY HUGE NEWS?

If you are new to my Drama Diaries, you're going to get the

wrong impression about Libby and me. We are not friends. I mean, I don't think we're friends. I mean, we are more friends than we used to be, but . . . Okay, the truth is—I'm a little confused about Libby and whether I can trust her. It was way easier when she was absolutely my worst enemy ever because she always acted like she was the only person ever born in Indiana who belonged onstage and it was totally annoying. Plus, she did some really mean stuff to make sure she got cast as Anne Frank and I didn't.

I think.

But then she was nice to me, too. Possibly.

The one thing I am certain about? She's excellent at taking what you are absolutely sure about and turning it upside down so that you suddenly start wondering why you ever thought it was right-side up.

So what am I supposed to think about this movie news?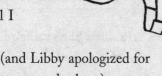

AAUUGGH!! A MOVIE! THIS IS HUUUUUUGE!

Okay, stop. (I'm talking to myself, not you.) I have to keep this in check until I really know what's going on.

Here are the things I am sure about (and Libby apologized for them so that makes me totally sure she meant to do them):

She definitely took out every copy of *The Diary of Anne Frank* script from every library in the county, and then she bought every copy at every bookstore anywhere around here so I couldn't study it for the longest time.

And she definitely swooped in and stole my moment with Rodney Vaccaro that time he was at the Franklin Hotel when he was showing the big-shot Hollywood location scout around Indiana.

But the worst one—the terrible audition outfit she tricked me into wearing—well, that's where it gets confusing, because she has all the right excuses for making it seem like she totally didn't mean for it all to turn out like it did.

But as Tammy (best friend and spokesperson) says, "But it did turn out like it did."

Which is true.

It certainly did.

Libby is in rehearsal for *Anne Frank*, which will open in Kokomo next month. And me? Well, I'm sitting here in my bedroom next door to my brother Chip's room, which is always filled with the sound of trombone-playing, and I'm trying to figure out my next move. Anyway . . . back to the email:

> And now for the truly GREATEST news!!!! Rodney says they are definitely going to be casting some parts here!!! Right in your hometown, Lainey! How lucky are you?! Can't wait to talk more about it. Gotta get to bed. Rehearsals are totally exhausting!
>
> xo,
>
> Libby

Rodney. She's calling him "Rodney" like they're best friends or something. And like I said, he is The-One-to-Know in Indiana. He usually works with the theatres in Indianapolis and he knows everybody and everybody knows him! Which means Libby is now way closer than me to knowing everybody, too.

And "rehearsals are totally exhausting!"? Does she really not realize that comment will totally bug me? To hear her talking about rehearsals when I wanted that part more than anything? It's just hard to know what she's really trying to do here. Is she being intentionally mean or just not very sensitive?

All this is why it's so hard to know what to make of this movie news and why she's telling me about it. No doubt *she* wants to be the actress who gets picked if there is a part for someone our age so why wouldn't she just keep the news to herself? Maybe she really has turned over a new leaf and does want to be real friends because we are (as she likes to say) the BYACI—Best Young Actresses in Central Indiana.

I want to scream and jump up and down because a movie is going to be shot right here in my tiny town, but I'm just not sure about what's really going on. I have to review all this with Tammy.

12 YEARS 4 MONTHS 8 DAYS

Tammy said, "I'm freezing."

Those were her first words after I told her about the movie.

"Will you focus?" I insisted.

"Yes, I'm sorry. I know. It's huge news. But when did it suddenly get so cold and why isn't the bus here yet?" She stamped her foot on the frozen ground. "Great. I can't feel my feet."

"It's not suddenly, Tam, it's December, and tell me what you think!"

"Well, it still feels shocking. Where is the downtown bus? Maybe we should do our Christmas shopping on the weekend."

"No, Tammy . . . tell me what you think about the movie!" I snapped.

"I think it might be warmer on the weekend," she said, shrugging her shoulders.

"Not about the weather!" I was crumbling with frustration.

"I think I'm glad they canceled school since they couldn't get the boiler to work."

"Not about the boiler, either!"

"Then what?" She looked at me like I hadn't said anything significant. I stared at her until she finally faced me with a totally different attitude and said, "Oh . . . okay, you want to know the truth?"

6

"Yes," I said—even though she was making me a little nervous.

"I'm staying distracted on purpose because I'm hoping you'll forget about this."

"About the movie?" I asked.

"About trusting Libby! About trusting anything she says! How can you forget all the stuff she's done?" Tammy's focus was dead set on me now. She wasn't even stamping her feet anymore. She just stared at me like I was the crazy one.

"So you're saying you don't think there's going to be a movie filmed in Fairmount at all?" I said. Wow. Honestly? I hadn't even considered that possibility. I was fully ready for there to be a trick involved, but it never occurred to me that the whole thing might be made up. "Wow. That is seriously depressing."

A REMINDER ABOUT SCRIPT FORM: Particularly important dialogue is put in script form so that it will be absolutely accurate when biopics (biographical movies) are made about me and my early days.

TAMMY

```
I'm just saying we better confirm this informa-
tion with somebody else who will know for sure.
Because whatever Libby is telling you, she's
doing it because it's gonna end up good for her
and bad for you.
```

"Well!" I laughed. "That's very quotable. That's going in the archives in script form!"

"Good!" She smiled. "At least then, hopefully, you will read it over and over and not do anything you're going to regret! Such as trust Libby Chamber!"

"I could call the Kokomo Players," I said. "They would probably know if there was a movie shoot coming to town."

A rumble came from around the corner. The bus was on its way.

"Finally!" Tammy said. "I don't think I have fingers anymore."

We had just sat down in the back of the bus when Tammy looked at me again with those really serious eyes. "Lainey?"

"What?"

"Promise me you won't email Libby back. She's tricking you. You know she is and . . . well, you know what I think."

I didn't want to promise that so I said, "Yeah, I know what you think."

"But do you promise?" Tammy insisted.

I nodded, but my fingers, toes, and most of my hair was crossed.

Later

FROM: LaLaLainey@yippee.com
TO: NanaFofana@ditty.com

SUBJECT: MOVIEMOVIEMOVIE!!!!!!

Nana!

I have the most in-cred-i-ble news ever! A big Hollywood movie is going to be shot RIGHT HERE IN FAIRMOUNT!! I found out from (and I know this is weird) Libby Chamber. She sent me an email with the news. Tammy made me confirm the news with some-body else because she's positive that everything Libby does is e-v-i-l. So I just called the Kokomo Players and this is what they said:

ME
I heard a rumor and I was wondering if you could tell me if there is definitely going to be a big Hollywood movie shot in Fairmount?

That's what I understand. I don't really know much more than that, but it certainly is what everybody around here is talking about.

Isn't it amazing, Nana! Talk about a great Christmas present! I'll tell you something that's absolutely, no doubt, totally certain: ALL I WANT FOR CHRISTMAS IS A PART IN THAT MOVIE! So keep your fingers crossed that some of the roles they're planning to cast here in Indiana are for twelve-year-old, blond, not-exactly-skinny PFPs!

Love,

Lainey, PFP!

I just finished designing this pin:

I SOOOO want to email Libby back. You know she's got more information. Plus, I know I shouldn't say this, but even if Libby isn't always the nicest—and by the way, sometimes she is . . . she can be very supportive—she does seem to know what's going on and being on her radar makes me more a part of the theatre crowd in Kokomo, which is not unimportant.

Yes, Nana has talked to me about "listening to my heart" or, as Mom calls it, "that voice inside" when I make decisions about who my friends are and how I should behave. But I actually am listening, and my heart says I'm not positive that Libby Chamber is 198% bad.

12 YEARS 4 MONTHS 9 DAYS

> **FROM THE DICTIONARY OF LAINEY McBRIDE:**
>
> CLIMB (noun): An un-club started by Lainey McBride as a reaction to the ridiculous clubs that girls start in sixth grade just to make other people feel left out. *Example:* The Movie Star Boyfriend Club started by Heidi Almighty at Fairmount Elementary. Lainey's belief is that joining a club is like saying, "I want to be just like U." CLIMB takes the U out of Club and inserts I M, which says, "I want to be just like I M."

It's Thursday, which means we had our CLIMB meeting at lunch today. I'm really happy that I started this un-club. So far we only have three members, but Tammy just designed the logo and I think our un-club is definitely going to grow.

Here's the logo she showed us at lunch today:

"If you don't like it, I have about ten other ones that I did," Tammy said.

"Would you stop?" I was smiling but firm. "This is totally perfect, Tam! You are *such* a good artist."

"It's really cool," Lenore nodded. "It works brilliantly on both a graphic and linguistic level."

Tammy and I both smiled a little bit.

"What?" asked Lenore, pushing her long black braid over her shoulder. "You don't think so?"

"No, I do. Totally." I laughed. "I totally think so. . . . What does *linguistic* mean?"

"Related to language," Lenore said. "It works as a picture and as words. That's what I meant."

"Ooooh," said Tammy. "Cool. Thanks."

I have to say, even though it was a terrible time a few months ago when Tammy and I fought over the ridiculousness of Heidi Almighty's stupid club, something good did come out of it.

Lenore.

If Heidi hadn't come up with her ree-donk-u-lus Movie Star Boyfriend Club that made everybody pick a Movie Star Boyfriend, and I hadn't insisted on picking someone none of them had heard of, and Tammy and I hadn't ended up fighting about it so that I ended up getting kicked out of Heidi's "gang"—then I wouldn't have ended up eating my lunch in the girls' bathroom and meeting the incredibly artistic and unusual Lenore.

"I wish I could draw or paint or whatever—I just don't have any kind of talent like that," Lenore said as she stared at the CLIMB logo.

And then there's that. It's so weird. Lenore can write a poem in her sleep. She can imagine whole worlds that don't exist (like during that phase when she was pretending her artistic father was the reason she drank coffee and moved around so much, when the truth is she hasn't hardly ever seen him). She can say things so they sound better than anything you've ever heard before. And she's truly smart—like, scary smart. Right now, her lunch tray is sitting on top of the fattest book I've ever seen (about the Renaissance . . . huh?). And it isn't because the table is too short for her to reach her lunch. It's because she's actually reading it.

She is a-m-a-z-i-n-g and yet—she's always putting herself down.

"I bet you have loads of artistic talent," Tammy told her.

The other thing? It is *such* a relief that Tammy and Lenore are getting along. It wasn't so great there for a while when Tammy realized I'd met a new friend during my time as one of the outcasts in the girls' room. (Turns out there's a whole universe in the girls' room during lunch that I never even knew about before this little episode.)

Anyway, Tammy and Lenore were a little jealous of each other at first . . . to say the least. But now that they've gotten to know each other, they've actually become friends!

"I seriously don't have any artistic talent!" Lenore insisted. "That's part of why I'm having trouble coming up with my I M Project."

> **FROM THE DICTIONARY OF LAINEY McBRIDE:**
> I M PROJECT (noun): An activity chosen by a CLIMBer that is designed to help the CLIMBer develop what is unique about them.

"Well, you're not alone." Tammy smiled. "I don't know what mine should be either!"

"Well!" I chimed in. "Mine is writing to Maeve Winkley until she writes me back and says I can audition to be a Divette."

"Divette?" Lenore asked.

I was a little shocked, I'll admit it, that with everything Lenore knows, she didn't know what a Divette is.

It just seems wrong. But I'm trying to be more understanding these days so I just said, "When Maeve Winkley does her stage show—as opposed to when she's being a movie star—her backup singers are called Divettes. I'm going to write to her three times a week. I won't stop until I get an answer and she says I can audition for her show!"

"That's impressive!" Lenore said.

"It's a perfect I M." Tammy nodded. "Wish I could figure out mine."

I was just about to help Tammy figure out her I M when Heidi Almighty and her groupies—Michaela and Susan—walked up to our table. They were all smiling a little too friendly-like.

"What?" Tammy smiled back because she is the best there is at being nice to everyone (except when it comes to Libby Chamber), no matter what.

"Well . . ." Susan giggled. "We just heard a rumor that there's gonna be a movie filmed here in Fairmount."

"Yeah." Michaela smiled. "We heard it's a big Hollywood one."

"We just wondered if you knew any of the details, Lainey. You know, since you're such a good actress and do all that theatre . . . stuff," said Susan. She seemed incapable of not giggling.

Heidi was smiling at me like she hasn't smiled at me since we were in fourth grade—back before puberty or whatever it was that made her turn from plain-old nice Heidi into Heidi Almighty!

"We want to be in the movie." Susan giggled some more.

Heidi nudged Susan softly to get her to shut up, but she'd already given away Heidi's real reason for being so nice. She was hoping I would tell her how she could get into the movie. Amazing! Now that Hollywood is coming to town, my love of acting and theatre suddenly isn't so stupid.

"I don't know anything, Heidi," I said.

That was actually true, but I could tell she thought I just wasn't telling her something because I wanted to keep it secret. That made me smile, which probably made it look even more like I was keeping some secret.

I gotta admit it. The whole thing was pretty fun—making Heidi so frustrated! But it also made me realize what I HAVE to do when I get home from school today. No matter what Tammy thinks . . . I have to email Libby and try to find out MORE!

FROM: LaLaLainey@yippee.com
TO: StarChamber@yippee.com

SUBJECT: re: Movie! Movie! Movie!

Libby!

Thank you for letting me know about the movie. You certainly found out first, but the word is definitely spreading. Girls at school who don't care anything about theatre are suddenly all interested in getting into the movie!

So, have you heard anything else? Do you know if they're going to cast any young parts here? Do you know who's starring in it? Do you know when it's happening or when auditions would be? Do you know who's directing?

Obviously, I'm interested in knowing whatever you might know. Hope you're good.

Lainey

FROM: NanaFofana@ditty.com

TO: LaLaLainey@yippee.com

SUBJECT: re: MOVIEMOVIEMOVIE!!!!!!

Lainey!

That is REALLY exciting news! A movie right in Fairmount! Do you think there might be a part for an old lady!? ☺

xo,

Nana

Apparently, everyone wants to be in the movies! However, at least Nana is actually an actress. Not the case with Heidi Almighty.

WHAT YOU SHOULD KNOW ABOUT MARTY . . .
but might not know if you didn't read my first volume.

(WHICH, BY THE WAY, IF YOU'RE A REPORTER OR BIOG-
RAPHER AND WRITING ABOUT ME . . . THAT'S JUST SLOPPY
RESEARCH. YOU REALLY SHOULD READ THE FIRST ONE
BEFORE THIS ONE!! SO, AS I WAS SAYING . . .)

1. He's a troublemaker.
2. He's a genius.
3. Two years ago, he was sent to boarding school.
4. Two months ago, Dad "was retired" from the army.
5. Marty had to come home because of "money problems."
Dad and Marty? Not such a great combination.

We are all sitting around the dinner table. As per usual—the new usual, that is, since Marty came home from boarding school—Dad doesn't look up from his food, Mom just makes sure everybody's plates are getting emptied (especially of anything green), and Chip continues his silent work of trying to disappear completely.

Then there's Marty, the only family member (besides me, of

course) who makes any noise. Marty makes endless noise. When Marty knows something, he talks about it. A lot. And Marty almost always knows something.

"So the thing that is so great about film is that you get a depth of image that you just don't get with video. There's so much more dimension with film, so many more interesting ways to play with the ligh—"

"Why are you suddenly so interested in film?" I asked Marty, knowing full well what his answer would be.

"That big movie you told me about, Lainey. Very cool, right? Got me thinking. Maybe I should talk to the director, see if I could work with him—not directing—I really don't think I'm ready to direct—but lighting, especially in film, now that's some interesting stuff."

"You can't just walk up to the director when you don't have any experience and expect to be able to work with him! You weren't even interested in lighting last week and now suddenly you know enough about it to work on a real, true, big-time Hollywood movie?"

I know I wasn't being very nice but I mean, come on! He's a little bit all over my territory. Right?

"I'm interested in whatever comes along, Lainey," he said.

"Unfortunately, he only stays interested until the next thing comes along." Dad barely lifted his head to get that one in. Then he went back into his silence and he took Marty there with him.

That's usually what happens. Marty is the only one who actually talks at dinner. (Sometimes I try to join him, but I don't always know what he's talking about because he goes into such detail about everything and skips around so much from subject to subject that it can be really hard to keep track of what he's talking about.)

Eventually, though, Dad will get annoyed and say something about Marty not being able to focus or not focusing on what he should be focusing on and then Marty goes silent, too. Then, all that's left is knife scrapes and fork taps.

After Dad said that to Marty, I started feeling bad about what I had said to Marty. I wanted to say something nice, try to make him feel better. But one, I didn't really want to take a chance of refocusing Dad's attention on me. And two, I didn't really want to get Marty going on another ten-minute monologue, because I think he was just about to start talking about how electricity plays into lighting, and once he gets talking about that kind of science stuff, he can go on anywhere from ten minutes to an all-nighter. And honestly? Third? I really do feel that any movie talk should come from me. I am the performer here, after all.

Almost makes me think twice about my other brother, the almost-totally-silent-except-when-trombone-playing Chip—kind of liking him a little more right now—at least he isn't trying to push me out of the way to get his own name in the credits!

Anyway. I say nothing to Marty or anyone else until I can get through the Brussels sprouts, and then the only thing I ask (beg) is, "May I please be excused?"

FROM: StarChamber@yippee.com
TO: LaLaLainey@yippee.com

SUBJECT: re: re: Movie! Movie! Movie!

I know, right?! This is going to be so amazingly cool! Oh, and by the way, I found out the title—*Broken Desert*. Isn't that a great title? Also, here's what Rodney told us tonight when we were on break during rehearsal.

(Pardon me, but am I alone in thinking she says "during rehearsal" way too much? Also, what's a Broken Desert? Okay . . . moving on . . .)

He said, "I got a preliminary list of all the roles that are going to be cast locally and I'm happy to say, you all have a shot at something!" So, I guess they are going to use lots of local people in some of the small roles INCLUDING one for the BYAC! Psych! Right? I'm not sure what the whole movie is about, but Rodney did tell me that the role that I'd be right for (you too, of course!) is the daughter of the lead character. The daughter is in THREE SCENES and has LINES! And she will need to look like she could be the daughter of the star, who is . . . (drumroll, please) . . . Craig Fortuna! So cute, right? Anyway, he's got dark hair and I hear he's pretty short so I guess that's a little bit of what they'll be looking for. But who knows? Anyway, I don't know any dates yet, but here is the number you have to call to get an appointment to audition: 555-7716. Rodney says the director's name is Michael Berkley. He's done some other movies, but mostly action stuff. This is his first drama. AAAHH!! So excited!

xo,

Libby

So how can I be mad at her? That's a huge amount of extremely important information right there! I will be calling that number in the A.M. as SOON as I wake up!

Only thing I'm kind of sorry about? Craig Fortuna. I mean, he's cute and a pretty good actor, but he's also Michaela's Movie Star Boyfriend! That stupid club had just started to kind of fade away. This is definitely going to bring it back . . . full force! (And, while we're on the subject, why couldn't he have blond hair like me? It'd be easier to believe we're related that way. At least Libby naturally has blond hair, too . . . no advantage over me in that department!)

Okay. It's 10:12 P.M. I can call in 9 hours and 48 minutes. Do you think 8:00 A.M. is too early?

Oh, and . . . when Libby says "short," do you think that was code for "she needs to be little like me—not big like you"?

> A REMINDER ABOUT SIGNS:
> Whenever something happens that makes it clear that I'm on the right path and truly destined for greatness, it's noted with a star!

If you ask me, it is high time for a SIGN.

NOTE TO SELF:
No midnight snack tonight.

12 YEARS 4 MONTHS 11 DAYS

I'm supposed to be meeting Tammy and Lenore at the bus stop to go downtown for more Christmas shopping, but I just had to record the fact that I called the number Libby gave me and it's a stupid message.

> STUPID MESSAGE VOICE
> You've reached the on-location production
> office for *Broken Desert*. If you are calling
> in regards to casting, please do not leave a
> message on this machine. Call back at a later
> time. Thank you.

May I just say, THAT is not a helpful message. I guess I'll just try again this afternoon.

Now I've got to run. I'm gonna be late meeting Tammy.

Just called again.

Message again.

I suppose it is the weekend. AUGH! I can't believe I'm going to have to wait until Monday to ask for an audition!

Meanwhile, Christmas shopping turned into clothes shopping in about 3.2 seconds.

I don't know why I don't learn my lesson. I just shouldn't try on clothes at stores when anybody else is with me. The ONLY time that didn't turn into a totally humiliating event was when I tried on the outfit that I ended up wearing to my *Anne Frank* audition. Even though I'm pretty sure that outfit hurt my chances of getting the part because it was bright green with big flowers and not black, like I had been planning to wear but didn't because . . . that's right, you remember—LIBBY CHAMBER.

ANYWAY! The point is—despite the fact that it ended up being pretty darn embarrassing on audition day, it actually was the only time I can ever remember standing in a store fitting room and being able to just pull on an outfit without using some real muscle, and looking in the mirror and thinking, *I look good!*

It was almost worth the audition embarrassment just to have that moment. Almost.

Unlike today, when everything I tried on made my arms look like overstuffed sausages and my stomach like a balloon.

Let me just say—I really don't think I'm fat. I know I could lose some weight, but the only time I actually start to think I'm truly fat is in dressing rooms.

I finally left Lenore and Tammy to keep trying on clothes and I went and got Mr. C. a CD of the new musical *Bonnie & Clyde*, which I happen to know he doesn't have even though he has an amazing collection of Broadway musicals. I got a DVD of a movie called *That's Entertainment!* for Nana—she'll just love it because it shows clips from all the old MGM musicals from the 1940s and 1950s. I also got Mom's special cream that she loves to use after she's been in potting soil all day at Fair Flowers. And I got Marty's Slugboy book. Personally? I think Slugboy is gross. But Marty loves it. He's read every one of them!

CHRISTMAS LIST:
MOM - Apple Annie Gardener's Lotion
DAD - Fishing Tackle Box
NANA - DVD of *That's Entertainment!*
MARTY - Newest Slugboy Graphic Novel
CHIP - Earplugs (Ha!) so he can play his
trombone without listening to my show tunes.
LENORE - Something black
TAMMY - Supply of newest Sculpey colors
MR. C. - CD of *Bonnie & Clyde*

Hold on. I'll be right back.

Okay. Just tried again. Message. AAAAAAAHHHHHH!

12 YEARS 4 MONTHS 12 DAYS

Sunday nights are my very least favorite part of the week. No matter what is planned for Monday, I get this dark empty feeling somewhere in the middle of me and, really, nothing I do makes it go away.

What I try to do is this: GET DISTRACTED.

Then, hopefully, I stop noticing that it's Sunday night and, if I'm lucky, I get tired enough that I can fall asleep without rolling over seventeen thousand times and turning the pillow over eighteen thousand times.

The stupid thing is this: It never fails that when I wake up on Monday, it's not so bad. It's just Monday, after all. So why all the hubbub? Beats me. But getting through Sunday night is not easy.

Especially when I'm waiting to make the MOST IMPORTANT PHONE CALL OF MY LIFE.

And also, ESPECIALLY, when I've stopped eating cookies. Which, by the way, was supposed to be my distraction—figuring out my new diet so that I can be smaller by the time my audition comes around . . . whenever that is. But the more I try to write down what I will eat for the next week, the more I think about what I won't eat for the next week and then it occurs to me that the best distraction I have from Sunday nights is to watch TV with a bag of cookies very nearby.

Sometimes it feels like everything in life boils down to the fact that I shouldn't eat as much as I do.

AAAUUGGGHHH!!!!!!!

I NEED A DISTRACTION FROM MY DISTRACTION!

I guess Mom realized I was in a bit of a Sunday-night funk, because the third time I walked into the kitchen before remembering that I can't have cookies, she said, "Why don't you write your letter to Santa?"

Now, FYI—I do know the deal with Santa. I mean, come on, I'm twelve. But it's a tradition in our family that you have to send Santa a letter or "he" won't know what to get for you. In other words, Mom needs suggestions. Whatever. I'm good with that. A little writing in exchange for a bunch of presents? I know a deal when I see it.

Dear Mr. Claus,

Greetings, Big Man. Hope this finds you happy and healthy this year. Hope the elves have things under control and the stress levels are manageable.

I'm just checking in to let you know I've spent a lot of time thinking about it and feel pretty certain about my list of requests.

Please know that I realize that not all these gifts will fit under the tree—not to mention, they are not particularly wrappable—but I hope that doesn't keep you from considering fulfilling my holiday hopes.

So, this year's list is as follows:
* The role of the young girl in *Broken Desert*
* A YES from Maeve Winkley to audition for her show
* A magic diet that will make me look like a naturally thin person like Libby or Heidi BUT that includes cookies and Skittles
* Turtlenecks in bright colors

* A video camera
* A straight black wig to add to my collection

    As I said, I understand some of these gifts are a little tricky. I tried to add a few more attainable items at the end. I will be very grateful for any of those items (and/or anything else that you might happen to think of). But seriously, I would never ask for anything ever again if you could give me the first three . . . even two out of three. Really, Santa. I've been a very good girl. No doubt! So please take that into consideration.

    Thanks so much.

        Sincerely,
        Lainey McBride
        PFP (Pre-Famous Person)

How great would it be if those first three things were really things Santa could deliver?

Very great. That's how great.

The recording.

Again.

Okay, tomorrow morning someone has to answer, right? Monday can't come soon enough!

Have I mentioned I'm not a big fan of Sunday night?

12 YEARS 4 MONTHS 13 DAYS

It is 1:34 P.M. I am in study hall right now. It's been a very dramatic day wherein I took the bull by the horns, show-business style, and didn't take NO for an answer. Since I don't want you to miss the drama, I'm writing these scenes LIVE-ACTION style!

Here goes:

"I didn't get a spot," I say to Tammy the second I get off the bus at school.

"What does that mean?" she asks.

She walks a little bit sideways and ducks her head down, trying to get a look at my face since I can't lift my head (seriously, I can't because I am so depressed).

"It means I called at 8:00 A.M.—I mean, I don't know what else I could have done! I called all weekend and nobody picked up and then suddenly at 8:00 A.M. on Monday morning there aren't any spots left? How is that possible?!"

Now I'm looking up. I'm standing in the middle of the walk that leads to the front doors of school. My arms are flying around because that's what they do when I accidentally start talking louder than I mean to which I guess means it must seem like I'm making a little bit of a scene because when Heidi Almighty walks by she says:

"Very dramatic!" Then she smiles like she's just kidding, but really? That was a slam. "So, Lainey," she keeps talking, "have you found out about auditions for that movie yet?"

That's when I guess I get even a little bit louder. I say something like, "AAERRRUUUUUH!" And I feel my feet stamping and my arms going up and down with fists at the end of them.

I don't see her until she is standing in front of me. Mrs. Patchuck, Principal Extraordinaire.

"Lainey McBride!" she snaps like a turtle. "I do not want to hear that there is more trouble with you! Heidi, are we having another problem here?"

SERIOUSLY!? When did I become such a villain in the principal's eyes? One passionate moment in the hallway a few weeks ago when all I was doing—honestly!—was defending Lenore and myself. I just told Heidi a few truths about who we are and who she is (like, we are on our way to very interesting lives and she will stay in Fairmount forever and do nothing).

Okay. So maybe it was a little harsh, but seriously, it's hardly enough to make me Public Enemy #1 . . . right?

"It's okay, Mrs. Patchuck." Heidi smiles really sweetly. "I think Lainey is upset about something, but I don't know what."

"Do you need to take a walk to my office?" Mrs. Patchuck is staring at me with her hands on her hips.

"No!" I say, and I can tell it comes out harsher than I told my brain to make it sound. "I just need an audition time!"

"What Lainey means to say," Tammy cuts in with her cue for me to SHUT UP, "is that she's sorry for the outburst, but she's had a very frustrating few days and she wanted to get it out of her system before she walked into school. It was Lainey's thinking that if she just spoke a little more loudly than she should"—and Tammy gives me a look like I ought to know better—"and let off a little steam by throwing her arms around"—she's looking at me again—"maybe a little more than she should in a crowded space . . . that things might go better once she is in class."

Okay. Now, seriously. That was brilliant. Right? I mean, let's just say it. The girl is good. Go, Tammy! I would never have thought of all that. AMAZING!

Mrs. Patchuck looks from Tammy to me.

"Is that an accurate assessment, Miss McBride?" she growls.

I nod and point to Tammy, like "what she said."

"Get to class," she finally says, and she steps out of the way. "The bell is about to ring!"

"Well, now—" I start to say something I shouldn't about how it wouldn't be about to ring if she hadn't gotten in our way!

"We're going!" Tammy shouts, and she grabs my arm and pulls me through the front door.

Tammy is still pulling me through the hall on the way to our lockers, but I need to tell her everything before the bell rings or I really might explode.

"The recording said, 'If this is a call about local auditions, thank you for your interest, but we are no longer making appointments.' I am quoting the message exactly, Tammy! I memorized it because I called it seven times in a row because I JUST COULDN'T BELIEVE IT!"

"I'm so, so sorry, Lainey. I can't believe it!" She opens up her locker and then opens up mine. "Put your bag away, get your books, and let's go!"

"Good morning." I hear Lenore's voice, but I don't look up. The depression again, it's making my head very heavy.

"I don't know what to do! I can't go to class. I can't focus. I can't go on," I say as I fall against the lockers.

"Uhhh," Lenore says, "what did I miss?"

"She somehow didn't get an appointment for the *Broken Desert* audition and now they aren't scheduling any more," Tammy says.

"What does that even mean?" I moan as I fall back against the lockers. "*Broken Desert*? Deserts don't break."

"It's clearly a metaphor," says Lenore. "Without reading the script, I can't say for certain, but my guess would be that it refers to war in some way—you know, like it's—"

"This is like the biggest UN-sign in the world!" I know Lenore is talking, but I have no idea what she's saying so I decide to be rude and just interrupt. I'm in crisis, after all. I am sliding down the lockers now so I can crumple up on the floor. "How do I put an un-sign in the Archives? How do I draw it? What's the opposite of a star?"

Tammy hands me my math book, closes both lockers, and takes my arm again.

"Lenore," she says, "get the other side."

They pull me down the hallway.

"We'll figure out something, Lainey," Tammy insists. "But you have to get a grip. You almost got in serious trouble out there. Mrs. Patchuck is not your biggest fan!"

"Right?" I say, stopping in the hall. "What is up with that?"

"A black hole," Lenore says. Totally random.

Tammy and I both look at her.

"That's the opposite of a star. I'm pretty sure."

"Seriously?" Tammy says, staring at Lenore like she can't believe she just said that.

"Great," I say. "A black hole in my Drama Diaries. That's gonna be really hard to draw."

"Math!" Tammy says, and she pushes me and Lenore through

the door of our classroom. "I'll see you at lunch!" she says, and she runs down the hall to her class.

"Hey!" Tammy is standing over me at the lunch table. Lenore is right behind her. They both hold lunch trays.

"Where's your lunch?" Tammy asks.

"What are you writing?" Lenore asks.

"I figured out what I have to do!" I am totally back on track!

"Okay," Tammy says, "that's good, but you also have to eat lunch."

"Not eating lunch today. Listen to this and tell me what you think." I pick up my notebook so I can read my speech word-for-word. "Hi, Mr. Vaccaro. This is Lainey McBride. Hopefully you remember me from the *Diary of Anne Frank* auditions. I had on green pants and a flowered shirt? I'm sorry to bother you, but I really, really want to audition for the part of the daughter in *Broken Desert*, and I haven't been able to get an audition time. Is there ANY WAY you might be able to help me get an audition? I know this is a lot to ask but I'm not sure what else to do and I want this more than I can possibly say! Thanks so much!"

I lower my notebook and look at Tammy.

"That's a letter?" she asks, chewing her macaroni and cheese slowly.

"No. It's my speech for the voice mail I'm going to leave for him on his phone at Kokomo Players. He really was nice to me at the audition even if he didn't cast me as Anne. I think he might remember me and be willing to help, don't you?"

"Yeah." Tammy nods.

"It's a good idea!" Lenore smiles.

"Except—" Tammy is looking at me funny.

"What?"

"Maybe leave out the part about the green pants and flowered shirt?"

I think about it for a second and then cross out the sentence. "Good call!" I say as I stand up.

"Where are you going?" Tammy asks.

"To get a pass so I can go use the phone in the office."

"But what about your lunch?"

"Not hungry!" I tell her.

Of course, that is a lie. I'm starving, but I'm not eating my lunch because (A) I have some extremely important business to do and (B) I have to get skinny!

I head for the door, a hall pass, and a solution to this great injustice!

Whoa! There's the bell and here's the end of this LIVE-ACTION segment! Pretty intense, right? I told you. It's been a very exciting day!

It's been twenty-eight hours since I left that message for Rodney Vaccaro and I haven't heard anything. I'm feeling sick to my stomach. It can't possibly be that the incredible, impossible miracle of a movie being shot right here in Fairmount is not going to include me being able to be in it. THAT CANNOT BE!

I was so distracted at my voice lesson today that Mr. C. finally gave up and sent me home early (which is unfortunate because we really should have been working on the three solo lines I have in the Holiday Concert next week). I just couldn't concentrate. I know. Not the focus of a professional performer. But I CAN'T HELP IT!

THIS IS EX-CREWWWWW-SHEEEE-ATING!!!!

Hold on. Just heard my email *ding*. I wonder if R. Vaccaro is emailing? He has my address if he still has my audition sign-in. Maybe Libby could get me his email and I could try to get to him that way. Maybe he didn't get my message. . . .

Be right back.

. . .

Okay. This is a little bit weird. Check this out:

Lainey,

I'm so sorry you didn't get an audition. I can't believe they won't take any more appointments. I mean, seriously, how is it possible that so many people are auditioning for a movie in Fairmount? Really rotten luck. I wish they knew you were one of the BYACI. I will try to tell them if I get a chance. Don't give up, Lainey. You're great!

xo,

Libby

So how does she know I didn't get an appointment? Is she so much on the inside of the cool theatre crowd now that she actually knows stuff like that? Did she somehow see the list of people who got an audition and saw that my name wasn't there? I feel so out of the loop. I hate this feeling! I should just answer this email and ask her if she has Mr. Vaccaro's email address, but something about that makes me feel even worse—like I don't have anything and Libby Chamber has everything!

It really doesn't feel like I've been alive long enough to be feeling as far behind as I do!

12 YEARS
4 MONTHS
15 DAYS

I HAVE AN AUDITION!

It went like this:

I'm in my room trying to figure out how to get Rodney Vaccaro's email without having to beg Libby. The phone rings. I stay in my room. Suddenly, Mom is calling for me.

"Lainey! You have a phone call!"

I'm not expecting a call. I pick up the hall extension. Curious.

"Hello?" I say.

"Is this Lainey McBride?" A lady's voice is on the line.

"Yes," I say.

"This is Cody Zelman, assistant to Pamela Chassin, the casting director on *Broken Desert*?"

I try to get myself to say "Yes?" or "I see" or "How are you?" But instead what comes out of my mouth is more like "Whagooshadobee?"

"We were given your name by Rodney Vaccaro, who spoke very highly of you as an actress."

I'm just going to repeat that if you don't mind.

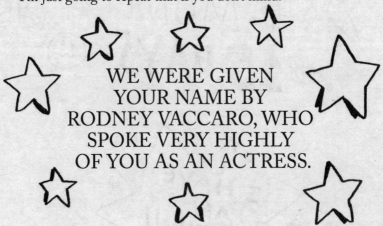

WE WERE GIVEN YOUR NAME BY RODNEY VACCARO, WHO SPOKE VERY HIGHLY OF YOU AS AN ACTRESS.

"Heeedigaboshee?"

At this point I'm just hoping that whatever is coming out of my mouth sounds better on the outside of my head than it's sounding on the inside.

"We would very much like to see you for the role of Olive. She's the daughter of the lead character who will be played by Craig Fortuna."

"Wow." I finally say something I can understand.

"Are you available next Wednesday at 4:15 P.M.?"

"Yes," I say without checking anything. Because, seriously, what wouldn't I skip, move, or blow up to make way for this audition?

"Wonderful. You can pick up audition sides on Friday at the Kokomo Players. And if you would, please also drop off a picture and resume at that time. Do you have any questions?"

I suddenly panic. "If I can't get a ride to Kokomo on Friday, would it be possible to email me the sides?"

(I mean how hard can that be? Sides aren't usually more than a couple of pages of your character's scene.)

"See what you can do," Cody says. "Pamela likes to meet people in person before she introduces them to Mr. Berkley, the director."

"Okay," I agree. "Absolutely. I will figure it out! Thank you SOOOO much!"

Cody Zelman laughs a little bit. I think she really likes me.

"Good luck," she says, and I can tell she's smiling. Then she hangs up.

FROM: LaLaLainey@yippee.com

TO: SculpeyGirl@yippee.com, SmartArt@yippee.com, NanaFofana@ditty.com

SUBJECT: AUDITION! WAAAA-HOOOOOOOOO!

Wednesday. 4:15 P.M. Me! Audition for Michael Berkley. Director of *Broken Desert*! How? Why? Because:

> WE WERE GIVEN YOUR NAME BY RODNEY VACCARO, WHO SPOKE VERY HIGHLY OF YOU AS AN ACTRESS.

Oh, yeah! That's right! He did! He said it!

I have to pick up sides on Friday in KOKOMO! Which, by the way, HELP ME! I need a ride! I'll take my bike if I have to, but if anyone has any ideas about something with a motor, I would love to hear it! YEEEEEEEEEEEE-HAAAAAAAA!

XO,

Lainey

FROM: NanaFofana@ditty.com

TO: LaLaLainey@yippee.com

SUBJECT: re: AUDITION! WAAAA-HOOOOOOOOO!

Listen, you silly girl, have you forgotten I'm coming tomorrow for your holiday concert at school? And make no mistake, come Friday afternoon, we will be in Kokomo to pick up those sides and see who we shall see! VERY EXCITING, my shining star!

XO,

Nana

12 YEARS
4 MONTHS
16 DAYS

"You were so totally brilliant to call Rodney Vaccaro!" Lenore said at our CLIMB meeting today.

"That was a good move." Tammy nodded.

"Well, I am officially redefining my I M Project from the Maeve Letter-Writing Campaign to Project Hometown Movie Star," I announced. "I can't wait to see the audition sides so I can really start working on specific character stuff. I want to walk into that audition and show them that I'm not just some kid they could cast because I happen to live in Fairmount. I'm a discovery!"

I stared at the lunch tray. I'd already eaten the beans and the peach slices. Everything else on the tray was definitely NOT on my diet. The mashed potatoes were sitting there just begging me to eat them, and the roll? I think the roll was actually smiling at me.

"Are you nervous about the holiday concert tonight?" Tammy asked.

"I am." Lenore nodded. "But I'm always nervous in front of people."

"It's just choir," I said as I picked up the roll and set it on Tammy's tray so it would stop smiling at me. "And you're in the third row. There's no reason to be nervous."

"Not everybody likes an audience, Lainey." Lenore smiled. "You don't want the roll?"

I grabbed it from Tammy's tray and handed it to Lenore before I could change my mind.

"So I think I'm starting to figure out my I M Project," Tammy announced.

"You are?" Lenore sounded really anxious, but it was hard to concentrate on what she was saying because I was so busy watching her pick apart the roll. Skinny people always eat so slowly. "I still can't figure mine out," she said. "I don't know what's unique about me."

That comment got my attention. I stared at Lenore with her long black braid and her extra-long legs and her beautiful brown skin and thought about all the amazing stuff she's said to me about books and movies and places I've never heard of. How could she not know what's unique about her? Before I could say anything to her, the bell rang.

"So I'll see you tonight," Lenore said.

"My nana is coming!" I reminded her. "You'll finally get to meet her!"

Lenore smiled and I just wanted to shake her until she woke up and realized how unique she truly is.

No matter what she chooses for her project, it'll be unique, because EVERYTHING is unique about her.

Well.

The Fairmount Elementary School Holiday Concert could have been considered a great success because:

    1. The sixth-grade chorus sang three songs and I had three solo lines.

2. Mr. C. said I totally nailed all three solos.
3. The applause got particularly loud when Mr. C. pointed me out after the songs were done.
4. Heidi Almighty messed up her solo line.

Plus, Nana met Lenore and thought she was really "interesting" and nobody got mad at anybody else at dinner. Soooo, it could have been a success BUT, unfortunately, it was not.

Because when I got home from school, Nana gave me a hug and said, "I brought you an early Christmas present. I saw it and thought it would look just great on you for the concert tonight." Then she opened her suitcase and pulled out a red blouse with little silver stars over the shoulders and down the sleeves. It was cool. I could see why Nana liked it. I held it up so Mom and Nana could see it.

"What size is it?" Mom asked.

That's when a funny look flashed across Nana's face and she said, "I'm not sure . . . it just looked right."

I pulled out the tag from the neck of the shirt. When I saw the size, I felt a queasy feeling in my stomach. Then I put the blouse down on the bed.

"Just try it on," Nana said. "If it looks good on you, what do you care what size it is?"

"Because it's a HALF!" I tried to not sound mad.

"It's a twelve," Nana said like she couldn't understand the problem.

"It's not a twelve, Nana," I corrected her. "It's a twelve *and a half,* and half sizes are only for fat people."

"That's not always true, Lainey," Mom said.

"Of course it's always true," I said.

"Just try it on!" Nana insisted. "It has got LAINEY written all over it."

I tried really hard to think of a way out of trying it on. But Mom and Nana just stood there, waiting. I felt bad for being so ungrateful to Nana, since she brought me a present when I wasn't even expecting one. But a half size? How could she think I would feel good about wearing a half size?

"Just try it on, Lainey," Mom said. "That won't hurt anything."

I wasn't going to get out of it. That was obvious. So I went into the bathroom and pulled the shirt on. I buttoned it up from bottom to top and then I just stood there for a while and stared at my reflection. I hated what I saw.

Me.

In a shirt.

That fit.

Perfectly.

And I'll tell you something. My mom was wrong. Trying it on hurt plenty.

12 YEARS
4 MONTHS
17 DAYS

We went to Kokomo in the Nanamobile. It is absolutely PER-FECT that Nana was here to go with me today to pick up the audition sides. Speaking of which—I pried a little theatre history out of her on the drive over.

"So how come they call them sides, Nana?"

"I actually just learned about that from a PBS documentary on Elizabethan theatre!"

"Elizabethan? That's Shakespeare, right?"

"Well, it's more than that, but it includes Shakespeare."

"So what does Shakespeare have to do with sides?"

"Well, apparently, because paper was not so easy to get back in the 1500s, actors were only given pages with their lines and cues and they called them sides."

"Because it was just their side of the story?"

"I guess so." Nana nodded with her eyes on the road.

"I could use sides when I'm talking to Dad . . . you know? So he could see my side of the story?"

Nana smiled. "But don't you think he'd have his own sides?"

"Good point," I said.

"Anyway," Nana continued, "sides saved paper and kept theatre companies from stealing new plays from one another!"

"There's the theatre, Nana!" I blurted out as I realized we were about to drive right by it.

It wasn't until we were parked and headed inside that I saw the poster. Well, truthfully? What I saw was Libby Chamber's face big as anything in the middle of the poster for *The Diary of Anne Frank*. I didn't want to look at it, but I couldn't keep my eyes from staring or my feet from walking right up to it!

"That's old news, Lainey," Nana whispered as she pulled my arm and got my feet unstuck.

"Old news that I can't get away from no matter what I do!"

"You are here because you have an audition for a feature film, Lainey! Keep your head in the game!"

I was really, truly trying to get my head in the game when the front door of the theatre swung open and Libby Chamber came flitting out.

"Old news?" I murmured.

"Lainey?" Libby suddenly squealed and threw her arms around me. "It's so good to see you! What are you doing here? Are you getting tickets for *Anne Frank*? I really hope you come see it. It would mean soooo much to me!"

I was so busy trying to get out of her grip that I couldn't even think about answering her questions. Why does she do this to me? I swear she isn't really my friend, but then she acts like this and I don't know what to do!

"Lainey is actually here to pick up her audition sides for *Broken Desert*." Nana's voice was really firm.

Libby's arms suddenly fell from my shoulders. "Really?" she said, and her voice squeaked a little. "I thought you couldn't get an audition?" She finally went quiet, waiting for me to say something—which I didn't. I just stood there like an idiot.

"Perseverance!" Nana declared. "Where there's a will, there's a way! You must be Libby. I'm Lainey's grandmother. It's very nice to finally meet you . . . put a face to the name."

"Um . . . hi." Libby seemed a little shocked, actually. It was like she was unsure of what to say, which I don't think I've ever seen before.

"We really do have to keep moving, Lainey. You don't want to keep them waiting!"

"They're waiting?" Libby was even more stunned. "Your audition is right now?"

"Oh—" I started to speak.

"The casting director just requested a look-see," Nana answered, and she pushed me through the door.

When I turned around to look at Libby, all I could see was this stunned look on a really pretty face and then the door shut.

"What is the matter with you?" Nana whispered once we were alone. "You just let that girl walk all over you! Why don't you take charge when she comes at you like that?"

"I just have trouble finding my words, Nana. I don't know why!"

"Because she is set on intimidating you and, apparently, she does! Did you notice how shocked she was that you have an audition?"

"That's because I told her—" I had to stop myself because the fact was I hadn't told her; she had emailed me and somehow already knew the news. "I don't know, Nana. I think she's just used to knowing everything before me and it caught her off guard or something."

"'Or something' is right. Come on. Let's get your sides!"

We walked through the doors that said Administrative Offices and the woman behind the desk said, "Lainey McBride, isn't it?"

"Yes!" I said. "How did you know that?"

"I remember you from the *Anne Frank* auditions. I'm so glad you're going to audition for the movie!"

I swear. It happened just like that. Like, who could write that better? It was the best moment I've had in a REALLY long time!

"If you'll have a seat, I'll let Pamela know you're here."

We sat down and Nana leaned in against me. "You take this moment, Lainey McBride! Don't you let yourself shrink!"

"Lainey?" a woman with a very friendly face opened the door beside the receptionist's desk.

"Hi!" I said. I popped up and turned back to Nana, who nodded but didn't get up.

"I'll wait right here," she said.

My stomach flipped as I realized she meant I had to go into Pamela Chassin's office all by myself, but I couldn't let myself shrink. I turned to Pamela, pulled back my shoulders, walked through the door, and started talking.

"It's really nice to meet you. Thank you very much for letting me audition for this. I'm so looking forward to seeing the sides. How are you? I like your shoes!"

Pamela Chassin laughed. "Thank you, Lainey. It's really nice to meet you, too! I just wanted to give you a little synopsis of the story so you have a better idea of where these scenes fit into the movie."

"Okay," I said.

"The story is about a man from a small town who is called up to serve in the Reserves and he's about to be sent over to the Middle East. He has made a lot of mistakes in his life and feels pretty much like a failure. Most of the movie takes place once he is in the Middle East, but it's very important to the story that we understand where he comes from and who the people are in his life. The part you will be auditioning for is Olive, his twelve-year-old daughter. She is a very strong girl who has often been the more mature one between her father and her. Do you understand that idea?"

I nodded. I was forcing myself to listen. For starters, my heart was pounding so hard it was tough to hear. But mostly, I just kept staring at Pamela Chassin and thinking: *She is a real live Hollywood casting director and she's right here talking to me like I'm a professional actress.*

"Do you have any questions?" she asked.

I shook my head. "No, thank you," I said. "I mean, no, I don't!" I smiled at her.

"I'll see you at the audition, Lainey. Thanks for coming in!"

We were headed back to Fairmount before my heart stopped pounding in my ears and my body started to feel like it was on earth again.

12 YEARS 4 MONTHS 18 DAYS

"Cue me again," I said as I stood in the middle of my room and faced Nana, who was sitting on my bed.

We'd been working on Olive's big speech for half an hour. The character is in three scenes, but this is the only one where she speaks. It's the scene at the depot where her dad is getting on the bus that will take him to the army base. He's about to go to a very dangerous place for a long time. There are lots of people waiting around. Olive's grandparents are standing nearby, but the focus is on the dad and Olive.

"Okay," Nana agreed, "but this time, I want you to think about what the casting director told you—Olive is like the parent and her dad is the child. How does that change the way you say these words?"

I nodded and shook out my body to relax. Then I looked down for a minute because that's what my acting teacher, Madame Ava, says to do before you begin a scene.

> *You must leave the world of the street*
> *and enter the world of the play.*
> *In order to do that, you must take a moment—*
> *for yourself and for your audience.*

I looked up and Nana spoke the dad's line:

```
It'll be better without me, Olive. You'll see.
You'll be better off. This whole town will be
better off.
```

I looked Nana/Dad in the eyes, then lowered my head just a teeny bit so my eyebrows rose up while I talked to her/him.

```
Look around, Dad. Look around! Do you really
think all these people showed up because they
think they're going to be better off without
you? They don't care about your mistakes, Dad.
They care about you and they know they won't be
better off . . .
```

This is when I took a little bit of a pause and, I have to tell you, I amazed even myself this time around. A tear ran down my cheek! A real tear! I continued the speech.

```
. . . and neither will I.
```

That was the end of the speech, so I stepped back a little and lowered my eyes. Nana waited a second before she said anything.

Then, finally . . . "Wow."

Real Tears!

"Wow?" I couldn't stop the smile on my face even though I didn't want to seem too impressed with myself.

"That was really nice, Lainey! You took my note and then did me one better!"

"What do you mean?"

"You were the adult all the way up to the last moment and then suddenly you were a little girl having to say good-bye to your dad." Nana smiled really proudly. "I think that's exactly what the writer wants that moment to be."

Sometimes when Nana says stuff like that, about my acting usually, it feels like I actually get taller . . . and thinner. It's weird, but it really feels like everything inside me rises up.

"Lainey? Nana?" Mom called up the stairs.

"Yeah?" I answered.

"Dinner is ready."

I sighed and felt that rising up start to lie flat; another family dinner when only Marty (and Nana) will speak. I sat down on the bed as Nana stood up.

"Aren't you coming?" she asked me.

I looked Nana right in the eyes and said, "It'll be better without me. You'll see."

For just a split second, she looked confused, and then she realized I just quoted the script. She let go a big laugh and pointed down the hall toward the stairs. "Go!" she ordered. "Now!"

12 YEARS 4 MONTHS 19 DAYS

Nana just left for home. Luckily, she's coming back on Saturday for Christmas. Life is just better when Nana is here, and rehearsals are definitely better when she's here.

I am not going to let that stop me, though. Lenore said she could help me rehearse after school tomorrow. I said YES! Because I've only got:

TWO MORE DAYS BEFORE MY FIRST HOLLYWOOD AUDITION EEEEEEEEEEEEEEEVER!!!!

I wish I could figure out what to wear. If I hadn't spent every last penny on Christmas presents for everyone, maybe I could get something new. But I can't. I can't afford a new outfit. And besides, it probably wouldn't fit, anyway.

12 YEARS 4 MONTHS 20 DAYS

It's a good news–bad news situation.

First the bad news—Lenore couldn't stay very long because, as she said, "I'm on duty at 4:15 P.M. because my mom has to work." (Lenore's mom cleans rooms at the Franklin Hotel, so she works lots of strange hours . . . like 5:00 P.M. to midnight and stuff . . . and so Lenore has to take care of her baby brother because even though they live with her mom's boyfriend, he says babysitting is not part of his job.)

Now for the good news—Lenore has been doing lots of research about acting and famous acting teachers; it's like she's a real director the way she talked to me during our rehearsal.

The first thing we did was my speech. Unfortunately, I couldn't get the tear thing to work today. (I wish I could take Nana with me into the audition!)

Anyway, I said the line and Lenore said this:

"You're watching yourself, Lainey."

"No, I'm not," I told her, then I said, "Wait. What do you mean?"

"Well, I took out a bunch of books from the library and I've been reading about that famous Russian teacher—"

"Stanislavsky," I said, because Madame Ava taught me all about him—except not all the stuff that Lenore seems to know.

"Right," she said, really intensely.

54

It's like watching a bigger version of Lenore when she talks about this stuff.

"Him and some other famous teachers, too. They all have different ideas about how to act, but there are some things that they all say. And one of them is that you have to be careful not to watch yourself when you're acting because that means that you're not really being the character. One director called it having a third eye."

I must have been staring at her, looking a little stupid, because all of a sudden she stopped talking and just looked at me.

"What?" she asked, and then she was nervous and back to regular size.

"Nothing," I answered. "Sorry. Didn't mean to stare. You just really talk like you know a lot. I didn't know you were reading all that stuff."

"Well, I wanted to be able to help you get ready and so I thought I would do a little reading, but then it got so interesting!"

She pulled her chair to the wall and leaned back with her arms folded. It truly felt like we were in a rehearsal hall somewhere. She was the director and I was the actress.

Lenore scratched her head. "Try the speech again. But before you start, use your imagination and make a picture of what your dad looks like standing in front of you and really see all those people standing around you.

"And don't just make it a crowd of people who all blend in together. Imagine what each of them looks like so that you are looking at specific people when you look around. And the bus. What kind of bus is it? And the weather. Is it hot or cold or raining or what? If you can make all that totally clear in your head, then you'll be too busy living in that world to watch yourself from this one."

I must have been doing that dumb stare again because Lenore said:

"Wha-a-t?!"

I shook my head. "Are you sort of, like, a genius?" I asked her. "I mean, seriously, Lenore. I think you should take that genius test because you don't think like any other sixth grader I know, and not to brag, but I think I'm pretty smart myself. But, *seriously*, let's just say, you know a LOT!"

"Let's just do the scene again, okay?"

I nodded. Then, I shook my body out. I looked down and then up.

I'm not saying I didn't see Lenore, but it was different this time. I could see a man, kind of short and with dark hair. His shoulders were pretty slumped and his clothes looked sloppy. His eyes were wide open like he was a little bit scared, but he was trying to smile like he wasn't.

Lenore's questions popped into my head as I started to feel the scene around me.

- What's the weather like? *Winter. Cold. Hard snow on the ground.*
- What kind of bus is it? *A Greyhound, and not a new one.*

I looked to one side of me. There was a mom-age lady with curly blond hair, staring at my dad. On my other side, there were a couple teenage boys with their hands shoved in their pockets like they were freezing.

```
It'll be better without me, Olive. You'll see.
You'll be better off. This whole town will be
better off.
```

Lenore was talking, but I was seeing a dark-haired man standing in front of me. He looked like he wanted someone to say he was wrong. So I said:

Have you looked around? You think this many
people showed up because they think it's a good
thing that you're leaving? They don't! They
don't think it's a good thing. They think it's
a really bad thing! They don't want you to go
and so they're trying to spend as much time as
they can with you before you leave. Nobody's
gonna be better without you. I'm totally not
going to be!

Suddenly, I had that same feeling I had in the middle of my *Anne
Frank* audition when I forgot my line. It was like I was crashing
back to earth. I looked at Lenore and she looked like she couldn't
believe what she just saw. Then she started laughing. Really hard.

"What?!" I demanded.

When she stopped laughing she said, "That was really great,
Lainey! I mean, you were seriously Olive and I could tell you were
totally in the scene, but the thing is, you still have to actually say the
words that are in the script."

"I didn't say the line right?" I asked.

Lenore started laughing all over again.

"WHAT?!"

"You didn't say the line at all, Lainey! But you said the right
ideas, so that's a really good start. That's how you're supposed to
memorize lines—first you make sure you understand the ideas and
then you find the words that the writer used to express those ideas.
I have to go home, but you should keep imagining all the stuff
around you and keep practicing that line."

"Okay," I said. "I'll do it in the mirror."

Lenore stopped at the doorway and turned around. "Stanislavsky
says you have to be careful when it comes to mirrors because you end

up watching what's going on outside yourself instead of inside yourself."

I'm sure I was staring again.

"You know?" Lenore asked like she wondered if I understood English.

"Absolutely," I finally said.

I don't know when it happened, but somehow Lenore went from being really, really smart to an actual full-blown prodigy.

CLICK!

12 YEARS 4 MONTHS 21 DAYS

Lenore may be a directing virtuoso, but Tammy knows how to keep me calm. They make a really good team, actually.

As soon as I got home from my voice lesson, I called her to come over. We had work to do. And fortunately for me, Tammy arrived with a mission.

"We will NOT be experimenting with your audition outfit!" she announced when she walked into my bedroom. "No bright green pants, no big flowered shirt!"

"You can stop bringing that up, you know. I'd be fine with that!"

Tammy keeps reminding me what a disaster it was to follow Libby's advice—partly because she doesn't want me to get in another jam thanks to Libby, but partly because she didn't like me following someone else's advice instead of hers. I'm not saying she doesn't have a point about Libby's advice, but I can tell with Tammy. When she's upset about something, it always comes out sideways and so you can never be absolutely certain she's mad.

For example, when I asked her if she had any more Christmas presents to get, she said, "I think Christmas has become way too commercial."

I had no idea where that came from.

"I'm just not that into it anymore. All the buying stuff and asking for stuff."

That's when she got up and went to my closet to start figuring out my outfit like she was so over Christmas that she was even over talking about how over it she was.

"Wow," I said. "When did you decide all this?"

"Don't you remember when we were little, Lainey? Remember when the lights would first show up on Main Street? And the big tree in the park with the Santa and reindeer? And Herpel's would make their windows look like it was snowing?"

"Yeah," I nodded. "They still do all that, you know."

"Yeah, I know. But it's not what we thought it was, Lainey. All the excitement and feeling like everyone was really happy?"

"Yeah?" I said kind of slowly, trying to figure out what she was really upset about.

"It wasn't true. Not any of it."

I stared at her for a second and then—

DUH!

The lightbulb in my head flashed like a lit-up Christmas tree. I'm such an idiot. It's so obvious. I feel bad. I'm her best friend. I should have realized it was going to be like this. This is Tam's first divorced Christmas.

And she's not going to talk about it. Not without a lot of help from her friends, anyway.

"I don't know, Tam," I said. "Maybe it's not that none of it is true . . . maybe it's just not as simple as we thought. Like *happy* and *excited* aren't the only feelings people are having, but that doesn't mean they aren't having those feelings at all."

Tammy pulled out a shirt, pants, vest, and shoes from the closet.

"Well, I'm not having them at all," she said as she laid out the clothes on my bed, one piece at a time. "That's all I know and I'm over it."

I nodded and said, "I know. I get it."

"ANYWAY!" she said, which means *this discussion is over*. "This"—she pointed at the clothes—"is a really good look for you."

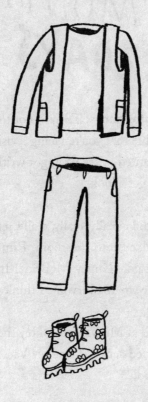

I've said it before and I'll say it again. The girl is good.

12 YEARS 4 MONTHS 22 DAYS

So, when you audition for things, it's hard not to notice that whoever is sitting at the table that you're facing is usually writing stuff down. I have always wanted to see what got written about me. But I've never been able to get a look.

Until today.

Let me just say—I did a really, really, really, really good job. NO DOUBT! When I walked into the room, Pamela Chassin came right over to me and said, "Lainey McBride! It's nice to see you again. Let me introduce you to everyone. I think you know Rodney Vaccaro."

I nodded and looked at Mr. Vaccaro. "Hey there!"

"Lainey is a very gifted actress," Rodney Vaccaro said.

Just like that. He said:

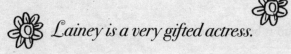

Lainey is a very gifted actress.

Any nervousness that was living in my body just evaporated. Why?

Because Rodney Vaccaro said:

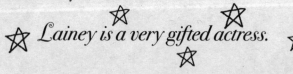

Lainey is a very gifted actress.

And that means I belong here auditioning for a big Hollywood movie. They want me here. I'm one of them.

Why?

Because:

Lainey is a very gifted actress.

All right, I'll move on.

"This is Michael Berkley, the director of the movie," Pamela said.

I felt so amazingly calm. I looked at Mr. Berkley, who, by the way, has really truly red hair and a very friendly face. I walked up to the table where they all were sitting and held out my hand.

"Hi, Mr. Berkley, it's great to meet you! I'm Lainey McBride and I'm auditioning for the role of Olive."

"Well, you look ready!" he said.

"I absolutely am." I nodded. Then I walked to the middle of the room, turned, and faced them.

"So you're in sixth grade?" Mr. Berkley asked, looking at my resume.

"Yup, and I'm still alive," I said.

They all laughed.

"Okay, Lainey. Do you have any questions?" Mr. Berkley asked.

"No," I said.

And then they all settled back in their chairs.

"I'll read the dad's line to cue you," Pamela said.

I nodded. Then I looked down, shook my body out, and when I heard Pamela's voice, I looked up.

All I can tell you is that it was everything that was good in my rehearsal with Nana and everything that was good in my rehearsal with Lenore. I saw my dad and the people and the bus. I felt the cold. I said the words that were in the script and, at the very end, a little tear rolled down my cheek.

And then I crashed back to earth. And Mr. Berkley's pen was moving across my resume while he stared at my face.

I smiled and shrugged my shoulders a little.

"That," Mr. Berkley said, and he stopped for a minute before he finished his sentence, "was really very good, Lainey. You live up to your reputation."

I think I know what it would feel like to walk on the moon. Like when those astronauts look like they're trying really hard just to get their feet to brush the ground before they float back up? Well, that was me.

"Thank you!" I said, and I felt a blush rising up in my cheeks. "Do you want to see anything else?"

"I don't think so, but thank you so much for coming to see us." And I could tell he meant every word!

I walked up to the table again, this time to shake everyone's hand good-bye, because Nana says that's a really classy move. I shook Rodney Vaccaro's hand. I shook Pamela Chassin's hand. And then, and I swear I wasn't even thinking about trying to get a peek at anything, I stepped in front of Michael Berkley and, before my eyes met his and before he shifted his hand so that it was covering the words he'd written on my resume, I saw what he'd written. Five words. Just five.

And for the second time in about sixty seconds, I felt like I was crashing back to earth.

I shook his hand and smiled really big. I didn't look back as I walked to the door and then pulled it shut behind me. My mom sprang out of her chair, staring at me hard with a great big

"WELL?" plastered across her face.

I kept my big smile on because after all that amazing stuff—after all those truly great moments and perfect feelings—all that I could feel inside me was a huge, gigantic sob . . . and I didn't want to let it out. At least not here. The five words?

GREAT FACE.
NICE ENERGY.
BIG.

12 YEARS 4 MONTHS 23 DAYS

"Enough with the silence," Lenore said as she rushed up to the lunch table, her hands full of lunch tray and crumpled papers. "You haven't said ANYTHING about the audition!"

"Right?" Tammy chimed in behind her. "I left you three messages last night and then you weren't on the bus. HOW DID IT GO!?"

"Sorry," I said. "I missed the bus. My dad had to drive me."

Lenore and Tammy both stood, staring and waiting for the real answer. But honestly? I didn't want to get into it. I'm embarrassed that he wrote that word on my resume.

"Okay, look," Lenore said, and she set her tray down, tossed her papers in the middle of the table, and sat down. "It couldn't have been as bad as you think. I saw you rehearse. There's no way there isn't at least one great thing you can tell us."

"How was the outfit?" Tammy asked, slathering butter on her roll. "Good look, right? Hey. Why aren't you eating lunch? It's the last day before vacation! They're giving out double rolls if you want them!"

"I'm not that hungry. And the audition went totally great. Probably couldn't have gone better." I nodded and tried to smile at them.

"Not getting it," Lenore said. "What's the problem?"

I stared at both of them and realized there was no way to avoid it. So I told them—how incredible it all was—how I did—what they said—what I said. Perfection . . . until the five words. Well, really, just one word. One word that almost certainly takes me out of the running for the part.

Big.

"It sounds truly amazing," Tammy said with a real smile.

"Totally!" Lenore agreed. "BIG is not terrible! It's actually incredibly important that an actor be larger than life!"

"The way Mr. Berkley meant BIG and what people mean when they say *Larger Than Life* are two different things. He meant my measurements—not my energy and attitude."

"How do you know?" Lenore asked.

"Because his other note said my energy was nice, so the BIG had to be about my body."

"Well, I don't think you should be so certain. You can't actually know exactly what he meant," Lenore argued.

"I think Lenore's right," Tammy said. "You don't know what he meant and it totally doesn't automatically mean that big is bad."

I didn't want to fight with my friends, but it's undeniable. *Big* means my body is big—big enough that he needed to make a note about it. That is so obvious it's sickening.

"What's all this?" I asked Lenore, and I picked up the pile of crumpled papers in the middle of the table. I really wanted to change the subject.

"Oh! It's for you—at least, one of them is for you! Mrs. Belter asked me to get these around school."

Lenore held up a piece of paper: the audition notice for the school play. I suddenly felt a weird combination of nervous, excited, and mad. I couldn't figure out exactly why I felt so mad right then, but I think I do know now.

I want to audition. Everybody will expect me to. But—and I'm being totally honest here—I feel so much fatter since yesterday and it pretty much makes me want to crawl under a rock. Anyway, back to lunch—

I shrugged my shoulders, nodded, and gave a small smile to Lenore.

"Oh, give me a break!" Tam said. "Don't be so depressed! Of course you're going to audition, and of course you'll get any part you want! You are Lainey McBride! I shouldn't have to tell you that!"

I stared at Tammy. It was shocking to hear that kind of bossiness coming from her. It was impossible not to laugh a little bit. Besides, she was right. No matter what, I'm going to audition, and I'll get a part.

Here's the flyer:

FAIRMOUNT ELEMENTARY SCHOOL DRAMA CLUB
ANNOUNCES AUDITIONS FOR THE WINTER PLAY

WELCOME TO THE CIRCUS HOTEL,
HOLLYWOOD DiVECCHIO!
Adapted by Howard Dewin

Sign-Up Deadline: Friday, January 7
Auditions: Monday, January 10

PLAY SYNOPSIS:
The play is set in an old condemned hotel, which is the secret home to a troupe of old circus performers. Hollywood is a twelve-year-old girl who has never felt like she fits in with her family and friends until she discovers a new family inside the hotel. As she finds her place in this crazy troupe of performers, she uncovers secrets they have kept for a very long time—some of which are about herself. But can all those secrets come together to save the old hotel when real-estate developers appear to knock it down?

LEAD CHARACTERS:

Hollywood	Sassy and tough. Requires a circus skill.
Hollywood's Mom	Understanding but firm. Moves like she was a dancer once upon a time.
Grandfather	Very old man. Once the greatest aerialist in the world.
Nel the Fat Lady	Wise and funny. Been in the circus her whole life.
Timbo the Strong Man	Rescues everything and everyone—even when they don't need it.
Twins Gymnastica	They only speak to each other. Must do gymnastics.
Jack the Lion Trainer	Older, but still handsome. Walks with a limp from an injury.
Olga the Wee Lion	Feisty and playful—likes to curl up in the nearest lap for a nap.

There are a few smaller parts available, too! So if you have any interest at all, give it a try! We have tons of fun and you will be very glad you got your nerve up to audition!

Please see Mrs. Belter in the music room to sign up and get audition materials.

"I know you want Hollywood, Lainey, but I hope you'll look at Nel, too," Mrs. Belter said to me as she handed me the script pages.

Mrs. Belter is really pretty and when she smiles at you it's really hard to say no to whatever she's asking you to do.

"Which one is Nel again?" I asked.

"Just read the scene." She smiled.

"Okay," I said.

It wasn't until the door shut that I remembered who Nel was. The Fat Lady!

Are you kidding? I thought. *Not in a million years!*

                    HOLLYWOOD
Why didn't my mom tell me I was from a famous circus
family . . . or how my dad died? Why did she pretend we
were just supposed to be like everybody else when we
weren't?

                      NEL
You found out a lot all at once today, Hollywood.
It'll take a little time to get used to all that new
information!

                    HOLLYWOOD
I'm trying not to be mad. . . . I'm not even actually
sure who to be mad at!

                     LOUISA
Lot of times, I just get mad at the way things go.

                    HOLLYWOOD
How can I be only twelve and have already missed so
much? I just want to go back in time and meet my dad
and see the Flying DiVecchios.

                      NEL
I know I seem older than the moon to you—but I used
to be much older!

                    HOLLYWOOD
Older?

                      NEL
It was a hot, sticky night in June a long time ago.
Wasn't sure we'd get through the show without somebody passin' out, but when we finally did, all I
wanted was to sneak back to my trailer and hide.
Couldn't sleep—tossed and turned . . . watched the
hands on the clock . . . dreading them all meeting
up at midnight.

                    HOLLYWOOD
Why?

                              NEL
It's silly—looking back—but it was almost my
birthday and I was filled with a great big sadness.
Tears rolled down my cheeks as midnight approached.
The more I tried to stop, the harder I cried. My
heart was aching. I wanted to do it all again. I
didn't want to move on.

                           HOLLYWOOD
I don't understand, Nel. What does this have to do
with me?

                              NEL
That was when I realized what makes you older and
sadder than anything else in the world.

                           HOLLYWOOD
What?

                              NEL
Being afraid that the past is better than what lies ahead.

                           HOLLYWOOD
But you didn't miss anything, Nel. You just wanted
to do it again. I didn't even get it once. I missed
everything.

                              NEL
We all miss things, sweetie, and then we get something else instead.

                           HOLLYWOOD
Nel? I was wrong about you. I'm sorry.

                              NEL
How so?

                           HOLLYWOOD
You're just—I don't know . . . I mean, you're
basically a normal person—

                              NEL
I am basically normal, honey. I'm just enormously
fat!

In my room. Just had a phone call. Pamela Chassin. I did NOT get the part. BIG surprise. But as she said, "Everybody just LOVED you, Lainey, and Mr. Berkley is really hoping you'll agree to be in some of the group scenes in the movie."

She didn't use the word *extra*, but that's what she meant. That's what I got. That's all I got. I'm extra.

Some Christmas present.

12 YEARS 4 MONTHS 24 DAYS

Nana just got here. It's Christmas Eve and now I know what Tammy meant. I'm not having any of those happy excited feelings either.

"I'm sorry, Lainey," Nana said as she sat next to me on my bed. "But you have to be happy about all the amazing responses you're getting about your acting. You have certainly impressed Mr. Vaccaro and you have to see that as encouraging!"

"Oh, yeah. I feel very encouraged. Encouraged to stay home."

Nana rolled her eyes. I knew the clock was ticking. She wasn't going to tolerate too much more of my complaining. It wouldn't be long before she turned into Wake-Up-Call Gramma, who is wicked honest and not worried about being nice while she tells you exactly what she thinks of your behavior.

"Did the woman tell you who did get the part?" Nana asked as she stood up and started for the door.

"No, and it felt weird to ask," I answered.

"You were right not to ask. More professional . . . but I wonder."

"Really?" I smirked at Nana. "Because I don't. Libby got the part. You know she did."

Nana scrunched up her face and held out her hand to me. "Well, never mind. It's Christmas Eve. Let's go eat!"

"I'm not really hungry," I said. And that was the beginning of the explosion.

I told Nana I shouldn't come down for dinner. I knew it was a mistake. But she insisted.

"Why aren't you eating, Lainey?" Mom asked the minute after I sat down.

"I'm not hungry." I smiled so it wouldn't seem like I was pouting or being immature.

"Well, at least eat your vegetables, okay?"

"No!" Dad suddenly barked. "Eat your dinner. I've been watching you push your food around your plate all week."

"I'm not hungry and I shouldn't eat if I'm not hungry," I said as quietly as I could.

"Well, I'll be darned if I'm going to sit here and watch you waste any more of the time and money that your mother and I put into making sure you have a good meal—"

"It's okay, Ed," Mom said softly.

"It is NOT okay!" Dad said, and this time his hand came down on the table and the forks jumped.

"Ed!" Nana snapped at him. "Behave!"

Marty snorted like he was trying to swallow a laugh.

"You think this is funny, young man?" Dad turned on Marty.

Marty shook his head and I could tell he was biting the inside of his cheek.

"Huh?" Dad pushed him.

"No!" Marty finally snapped. "I don't think it's funny when you act like a dictator!"

I heard Chip sort of exhale, and he started to slide down in his chair. Dad stood up and his chair slid halfway across the kitchen floor. Marty's whole body looked coiled, and Mom's head was snapping from one person to the next.

"Ed McBride!" Nana roared over all of it. "Knock it off! It's Christmas Eve! Can't this family even enjoy each other for twenty-four hours?!"

Dad's face was red and he looked like one of those caged lions that paces back and forth at the zoo. Finally, he turned his head away like he was too disgusted by us to even look at us, and he walked out of the room. We all sat really still until we heard the side door close and we knew he was back in the garage at his workbench.

"May I please be excused?" Chip asked in a totally flat tone.

"What he said," Marty said, and he sounded like he hated everyone in the entire house.

Mom nodded. She didn't speak and I was afraid she was going to cry.

"You too, Lainey," Nana said in a whisper. "As long as you're not going to eat why don't you head up to your room."

I was the last one out of the kitchen and I know I shouldn't have, but I stopped once I was out of view.

"You okay, Louise?" I heard Nana ask Mom.

There was a quiet pause, but then I heard Mom take a deep breath. "It's the money. All this Christmas business has made it impossible to ignore. Ed needs to figure out what he's going to do now that he's done with the army . . . or as he says, 'now that the army's done with me.' I don't know what to do."

I heard Mom make a funny noise and it took a second to realize that she was actually crying. My feet took me toward the stairs. Even though my brain really wanted to hear what else was going to be said, my body knew it wasn't going to feel good once I heard it.

12 YEARS 4 MONTHS 25 DAYS

Merry Christmas.

I ate half a nut-roll that Nana made, a chocolate Santa from my stocking, scrambled eggs and hash browns, turkey, stuffing, green-bean casserole, cinnamon Jell-O salad, mashed potatoes, seven Christmas cookies from the plate the neighbors brought over, and a slice of pumpkin pie.

Okay, two slices of pumpkin pie.

But you have to eat the good stuff on Christmas, right? Besides, I was just trying to keep the peace and not create another not-eating-food-related family explosion.

Either way, I'm surprised and pleased to report that even though life has not been exactly holiday happy recently, that Christmas Thing happened. There's just something about Christmas—no matter what you're thinking might happen or could happen or should happen—it ends up being a special day.

Like, for example, I didn't have trouble falling asleep last night like I always have on Christmas Eve, and that actually made me feel pretty sad while I was lying in my bed. BUT this morning, I woke up at 5:14 A.M. and no matter how hard I tried, I couldn't fall back to sleep. I was just too excited. It was like my internal RESET button got pushed while I was sleeping.

I ended up sitting on the stairs for two hours. It's a family rule

76

that we aren't allowed to go downstairs on Christmas morning until everybody is up and ready. So if you wake up at 3:00 A.M., you just have to sit and wait.

Example two: Chip showed up on the step next to me at 5:39 A.M. and Marty sat down on the stair behind me at 6:11 A.M. We didn't say much to each other, but it felt pretty great to all be excited together, like we used to be when we were all little.

Examples three, four, five, and six: When Dad woke up, he came out into the hall and said, "What's going on? You all think there's something downstairs that's going to bite you?"

That's Dad's version of a joke.

When we ran down the stairs and into the living room, it was shocking how many presents there were.

Mom said, "I guess Santa really did come after all."

And I gotta tell you, I almost believe her, since I know we don't have any money these days, so how is it possible that Mom and Dad would have bought all these presents?

When Chip opened up his present from me (earplugs), he read the note I had stuck inside—

These are so you can practice your trombone without hearing my music!

He actually laughed and said, "I'm really gonna use these, Lainey! Thanks!" And you could tell he thought it was funny by the way he said it. I'm talking *expression*, people. Chip actually had expression in his voice!

77

And at Christmas dinner, Dad didn't shout, Marty didn't sulk, Nana didn't scold, and everybody was still in their seats at the end of dessert.

It's like Christmas pushed everybody's RESET button. I'm really hoping the RESET button was hit at Tammy's house, too.

12 YEARS 4 MONTHS 26 DAYS

Nana was packing her bag when I heard the ding. Incoming email. I knew the second I saw it what it was going to say. I read it and printed it out.

"Nana," I said as she headed down the hall with her bag.

"Yes, madam," she replied.

"Look," I said, and I handed her the email.

FROM: StarChamber@yippee.com
TO: LaLaLainey@yippee.com

SUBJECT: Wanted to let you know . . .

Hey Lainey,

I just wanted to tell you myself that I found out right before Christmas that I got the part in the movie. I know you auditioned, too, so I'm hoping that hearing it straight from me is easier than hearing it from someone else. I know you did GREAT in your audition, but you know how this stuff goes. It's just about "type" and sometimes you win and sometimes you lose. Hope you had a great Christmas. Maybe we can get together over vacation. That would be really fun.

Ciao for now!

Libby

When Nana looked at me over the top of the paper, I knew she was done reading.

"Told ya!" I declared.

"It doesn't change all the positive feedback you are getting. Forget about her and PLEASE do not respond to this email and PLEASE, PLEASE do not get together with her. You do know she's not your friend, don't you?"

I nodded and kind of shrugged.

"She knows you are her biggest competition and she is always trying to keep you from succeeding."

"I know, Nana. But you're the one who told me to keep my friends close and my enemies closer."

Nana laughed and shook her head.

"I can handle Libby," I reassured her. "Don't you worry."

"Yeah. I've seen how well you handle her!" I knew Nana was going to mention that—the way I froze up in front of the theatre when we ran into Libby about a week ago.

"I was just caught off guard that time. . . ."

"In any case! You have an audition to prepare for. You should be doing some research on the circus!"

"You're right." I tried to stop her. "Do you really have to leave? I picked up the audition scenes and monologues before school got out on Friday. We could work on them together."

"And we shall, but first, you have to do your homework on the script! Christmas vacation is a perfect opportunity to find a spot in the library and read everything you can about the circus. There's some interesting history there, you know."

"Okay." I reached for Nana's bag.

"What?" she snorted. "You think I'm an old lady who can't carry her own bag?" She pulled the bag out of my reach and headed down the stairs. But before she got to the bottom she turned back and looked me in the eye.

"Lainey?" she said, and it was her "listen to me and listen good" voice.

"Yeah?" I responded.

"Cut the no-eating business. It's ridiculous. It doesn't work. And it's a dangerous game."

She didn't wait for me to answer. She just turned and disappeared around the corner, headed for the front door.

12 YEARS 4 MONTHS 27 DAYS

"Fair Flowers. Good morning. This is Lainey. How can I help you?"

Now repeat that twenty-seven times and you'll know what I've done since 8:30 this morning . . . and (because I promised Mom) what I will be doing for the rest of the day and maybe for some other days this week!

Mom says she can get a ton more work done if she just stays focused on the floral arrangements. So I told her that as part of her Christmas present, I would help at the shop this week.

She liked the lotion I got her, but she loved the help offer even more. Probably the most successful present I gave this year.

Wish being here wasn't sooooo boring. Although it's not so boring when people actually come into the shop and I get to wait on them. It's just that, mostly, it's answering the phone or . . . waiting to answer the phone.

We did stop at the library on the way over here, however, and I got a very cool book on the circus. It's called *The Big Top Train*. It's all about how the circus used to be when the entire thing (elephants, tigers, horses, high wire, clown cars, bleachers, all the people, all the food, all the costumes, all the EVERYTHING) used to get packed up on big long trains and travel from town to town.

When that train pulled into a new town, the workers would get everything unloaded and set up all the tents and equipment.

82

There would be a huge dining tent with an amazing kitchen. There were costume tents, dressing-room tents, mechanical and carpentry tents, performer tents, livestock tents, and even a hospital tent. And, of course, there was the BIG TOP!

It was like the circus family (which was a LOT of people) was always in its own little town and it was located inside a bigger town that changed every few days!

I have to say . . . it seems really cool. I can see why it might be necessary to run away and join the circus. I'm going to have to do some more research on this.

Here are a few interesting circus facts for you:

1. Jumbo was an elephant that P. T. Barnum brought to America in 1882. That is when the word JUMBO started to be used to describe anything really huge! (BTW, he weighed thirteen thousand pounds, so at least I know I'm not JUMBO!)

2. In 1892, a circus food booth ran out of sausage links so they made patties from ground meat. That was the first hamburger!

3. Circus contortionists are either "frontbenders" or "backbenders" depending on which way their spine is most flexible.

4. Enterology contortion is the ART of squeezing your whole body into a really teeny box. (Bet you couldn't do it if you were JUMBO!)

I know. These are not really the kinds of things I'm supposed to be researching, but can I help it if I happen upon these little tidbits as I read? I mean, come on! It's interesting. Makes you wonder things you've never wondered before.

For example, I wonder if it's more common for an enterologist to be a frontbender or a backbender.

Acting is such an interesting profession. You get to learn so much.

Another interesting thing I learned is that there is NO WAY I want to audition for the part of Nel!

I read about this one woman called Baby Ruth and she weighed 815 pounds. She weighed 16 pounds when she was born and by the time she was ten, she weighed 300 pounds. One time, when she went to the hospital to have surgery, they couldn't operate because the table she was lying on collapsed. And the pictures of her? Well. I don't even want to discuss it. Let's just say, I do NOT want to play that part!

Oops. Gotta go. An actual customer just walked in!

So, wow! I just made a REALLY big sale! Mom is very happy with my sales skills. Although I have to say, I didn't really do anything. This woman with long dark hair and a really cool leather jacket and a phone that NEVER stopped beeping just walked through the door and came right up to me at the front desk.

"I need six large arrangements," she said. It wasn't that she wasn't nice, it's just that she didn't really seem to want to spend a single second more on any one thing than was necessary. She only looked up from her phone about every third sentence.

"Okay. Well," I said, trying to be really professional, "would you like to select from our arrangements in the case or do you have something else in mind?"

Good, right? I was smooth.

It didn't even seem like she looked in the case. She just said, "These need to be impressive both in size and arrangem—" She looked up from her phone and, I think, just noticed I was twelve. "Would it be possible for me to talk to . . ."

"I'm going to get my mom," I said.

"Perfect!" The woman smiled and she went back to her fancy phone.

"What can I do for you?" Mom popped out from the back like she'd been waiting for her cue.

The woman did some more of her fast talking and Mom took notes and nodded a lot. She showed her some different flowers and vases and after about ten minutes, Mom put down her notepad.

"When would you like these?" Mom asked.

"Wednesday," the woman said, "but I will need to call you with the delivery address. Can we take care of payment now?"

"Uh." Mom was getting a little flustered. "Well, I don't really know how much it will be yet. I need to sit down and add things up. Let me just go in the back and—"

"I really have to run," the woman said. "Can we just put a charge through on my card for six hundred—call it a deposit—and then we can settle up the rest upon delivery?" The woman handed Mom her credit card.

I could tell Mom was shocked. Her eyes weren't doing much blinking and it was taking her a while to say any words.

"No?" the woman said.

"No." Mom shook her head. "I mean yes. That would be absolutely fine. They'll be ready on Wednesday and I'll deliver them as soon as I hear from you!" Mom ran the woman's card and quickly handed it back.

"Perfect!" The woman took a card from the holder on the desk.

"Thank you, Louise," she said, reading my mom's name off her card. Then she was out the door.

"Well, that was a decent sale." I smiled at Mom.

Mom laughed. "I guess! You are quite a saleslady, Lainey!"

"I think we should talk about a raise," I said.

"That deposit is more than I would have figured the whole order would cost. I've got to figure out how to make these arrangements really amazing."

"Do you know who that woman is?" I asked Mom.

"Just that her name is Alice Glenn. That's what her credit card said."

"I don't think she's from Fairmount," I said.

"I do believe you are right about that, Lainey! I do believe you're right." Mom was a little spaced out as she walked toward the back room. I think she was trying to figure out how to make an arrangement that would cost as much as that lady wanted to spend.

"We can talk about my raise later, Mom," I said to her back.

She didn't answer.

12 YEARS 4 MONTHS 29 DAYS

I'm such an idiot! Why didn't I just agree to help Mom in the flower shop for ONE MORE DAY? Why didn't I put two and two together and figure out that when a cool lady swishes into a Fairmount, Indiana, flower shop and drops $600 without batting an eye at the same time that big-time Hollywood people are about to show up to shoot a movie—that the two are probably related?!

I'm sure you've already figured out what I missed by staying home to watch really important reruns of *Nanny and the Wizard*. That's basically what I did all day. I claimed the couch and watched thirty-two episodes in a row. (That may be a slight exaggeration.)

In any case, meanwhile, the lady called back and said the flowers should be delivered to 274 S. Mill Street, Apt 3. Mom loaded up her amazing arrangements in the car and drove to the address. She carried the first arrangement up to the door and rang the buzzer numbered "3." She got buzzed in and when she found the door with the "3" on it, apparently there was a sign taped to the door that said:

BROKEN DESERT PRODUCTION OFFICE

PLEASE KNOCK!

Mom said she was just about to set the arrangement down so she could knock when the door swung open and Alice Glenn was standing there.

Mom says she just stared at the arrangement for a while, and Mom was really, really scared that she hated it. But then she said "WOW!" extremely loudly, called Mom brilliant, and asked if the rest were just as stunning.

Mom didn't even have to unload the rest of them. Alice had some PAs do it. (Don't worry. I had looked that up. PA = Production Assistant.) I guess she got more excited with every arrangement that was brought into the office.

"I've got people showing up starting tonight and these are going to be just perfect in their hotel rooms when they arrive. Thank you so much!"

My mom is a genius.

Clearly, I am not, since I COULD HAVE BEEN IN THE PRODUCTION OFFICE! I COULD HAVE MAYBE SEEN WHO'S SHOWING UP WHEN. MAYBE FIGURED OUT ANOTHER WAY TO GET A REAL PART IN THE MOVIE! **AAUUGGHHH!**

12 YEARS 4 MONTHS 30 DAYS

We hadn't planned on having a CLIMB meeting this week, but I called an emergency session to discuss the fact that we now know where the big Hollywood production office is and SHOULDN'T WE TAKE ADVANTAGE OF THAT FACT?!?!?

"Actually that works perfectly for me," Tammy said. "I finally figured out my I M Project, and knowing the address is the last piece of the puzzle!"

"What are you talking about?" Lenore asked.

"I'm going to give each of the movie's stars a Sculpey of themselves to thank them for coming to Fairmount. I'm so psyched to have some new people to make them for, because I've kind of run out of people around here! The problem was, I didn't know how I would get them to the actors. Now I do!"

"We'll just deliver them to the production office!" I announced. "Nice! Now how can we use this to get me a real part in the movie?"

"That's a good project," Lenore said to Tammy. She was working really hard to be happy for Tammy even though I could tell it bugged her even more that she hadn't figured out a project for herself.

"This is Craig Fortuna!" Tammy pulled out a very cool figure— one of her best, if you ask me!

"Oh, he's great!" I said supportively. Then, "But does anyone

Craig
Fortuna

have any ideas about me getting a real part?"

"Now I just have to do Debi Buslik, Amy LeBlanc, and Rod Dugas. Do you know any other actors that are coming into town?"

"That's all I've heard," Lenore said. "My mom has been sneaking looks at the reservation book at the hotel. So far, she hasn't seen any famous people's names."

"I LOVE that your mom can do that!" I announced. "It totally gives us the inside scoop! Might be another way to get me in the movie? Hello?"

"Yeah," Lenore nodded, "I guess it is cool." Her smile was a little wobbly, like she wasn't used to thinking it was cool that her mom cleans rooms at the hotel.

"So," I said, "is anyone going to answer my question?"

Lenore and Tammy looked at me like they had no idea what I was talking about.

"Getting me a part in the movie! We have the production office address and we have the inside scoop at the hotel. How do we use that information to get me a part?"

I stared at both of them, waiting. They both stared at me, blank. "Sorry," Tammy finally said, "I got nothing . . . but I'll keep thinking about it. Okay?"

"Yeah," Lenore agreed. "Me too."

Well, what can you do? When your handlers come up empty-handed, they come up empty-handed. I decided to change the subject.

"Hey, Lenore. What have you thought about for your I M Project?"

"I've thought of a lot of things, but nothing is really THAT thing. You know?"

I nodded even though I did know what *that* thing was. I've always known. I can't imagine not knowing what you REALLY want to do with your life. I mean, I don't know exactly how I will do it, but I've always known what I want to do.

"You'll figure it out." Tammy smiled at Lenore and then she stood up. "I'm sorry, guys, but I have to be home in twenty minutes. My dad is picking us up to take us out to dinner."

"Oh," I said, and I made a face. Tammy smiled, but it wasn't a very happy smile.

"Talk to you later," Tammy said as she headed down the stairs and out the door.

I turned back to Lenore, who was looking at the script for *Hollywood DiVecchio*.

"What part do you want?" she asked.

"Hollywood, of course!"

"I know she's the title character, but I actually think the Fat Lady is the most interesting role," Lenore said, totally seriously.

"I am NOT playing the FAT Lady!" I told her.

"Just asking," she said, looking up from the script. "Are you ready?"

"Not yet," I said. "But I've been working on it."

"Show me," she said, and suddenly, that thing happened again. She went from being regular-size Lenore to being bigger-than-life Lenore . . . maybe even JUMBO size!

"Just remember," she said after the first time I read through as Hollywood, "acting is reacting."

I've heard that before, but never fully got it. The way Lenore said it—it just made sense.

"Hollywood does a lot of listening in this scene, but that doesn't mean you aren't part of the conversation. Listening is more important than talking most of the time. But you have to do it so that the other actors and the audience know what you're feeling and thinking about the things you are hearing."

The next time we read through the script it was like a million and three times better.

12 YEARS
4 MONTHS
31 DAYS

Interesting find today, people. Very interesting.

I went to Muncie with Mom. She had to deliver flowers to a New Year's Eve wedding, so I got her to agree to drop me off at The Play's the Thing so I could see what Mr. Mankewicz might have in his store for circus performers.

"No more than a half hour, Lainey," Mom called out the window of the car as I opened the door to the store.

"I know, I'll be ready." I waved at her.

Then the door shut behind me and I got that blast of smell that only exists in this store and in the basement dressing room of the Kokomo theatre. I guess it's a combination of theatre makeup, dust, and air that hasn't moved since about 1972. I really don't know what creates the smell, but it makes me so happy inside, and in such a calm way. I just feel this wave of perfect contentment whenever I'm in there.

"Lainey McBride," I heard Mr. Mankewicz say before I even saw him. "You survived the rejection, I see."

"And you are as cheerful as ever, I see," I said back to him—kind of surprising myself—but then I saw him almost smile. I guess most people don't bother to tell him he's cranky. "No, I didn't get the part of Anne Frank."

"I know. I saw the flyer with that Chamber girl," he pointed to a stack of postcards sitting on his checkout counter and I saw a little sneer run across his face.

"I'm already on to several new projects," I told him. (That's the way Maeve would say it.) "In fact, that's why I'm here. I'm researching circus people for an upcoming audition. I need some props and makeup and anything else that might help me to explore that world."

"There are some clown elements in with the makeup, but any circus folks I've known build their own props and set pieces because they know exactly what they need for their act."

"Interesting." I nodded.

"You'll have to look around," he said, shooing me off. "You're the only one who could know if something works for your character or not."

"You are so right about that, Mr. Mankewicz," I said. "You must be a very good actor."

He kind of rolled his eyes when I said that, but I think, secretly, he was pretty pleased to hear me say it.

I spent about five minutes trying on clown noses and wigs. (I love wigs!) Then I moved up the aisle to the makeup and put on some glitter eye shadow and one beauty mark. I went back to the lighting section and looked at all the different color gels. I walked back up the shoe aisle and ran my hand over the tops of all the tap shoes.

Then I was in the costume elements aisle. Mr. Mankewicz has a great collection of uniforms—policeman, fireman, doctor, nurse, maid—tons of different possible character outfits all hanging on a rack. I flipped through all of them, until I came to one that had me stumped.

It was basically a shirt, but it was packed with foam. I took it off the rack and then I realized what it was. A fat suit! Ugh! I jammed it back on the rack and walked quickly down the aisle. I'm so glad nobody saw me holding that. It's bad enough being big. I don't want to look stupid, too—as if I haven't figured out that I don't need to wear one of those to look fat!

"Hey!" Mr. Mankewicz shouted from the front of the store. "It's almost a half hour since you got here. Didn't your mother say to be ready in a half hour?"

"Yes!" I said as I hurried toward the front of the store. "Thanks."

I looked out the front door, but my mom's car wasn't there yet. Mr. Mankewicz was behind the counter.

"Sorry I'm not buying anything," I said, "but I'm actually going to follow your advice and get my dad to build me some stilts. I tried walking on some once at my cousin's house and was pretty good at it. I think that would work, don't you?"

"Suit yourself," he said as he straightened the stacks of post-cards and flyers that sat on the counter—including, of course, the postcard for *The Diary of Anne Frank* with Libby Chamber's face plastered across it.

"She is a pretty girl," Mr. Mankewicz muttered.

"I know." I nodded.

"Pretty counts," he said without looking up from his papers.

"I know!" I said. "I don't need to talk about this anymore. Do you?"

He laughed a little and said, "Suit yourself."

He went back to his paperwork and I stared out the window, looking for Mom's car.

"You audition for this?"

I turned back to Mr. Mankewicz, who was pointing to a flyer that had been pushed off to the side—the audition notice for *Broken Desert*.

"Yes," I said, really wishing I didn't have to tell him I didn't get that one either. "I'm in some of the group scenes."

Mr. Mankewicz nodded. I waited for a wisecrack about being an extra, but none came.

I looked more closely at the audition flyer. I hadn't ever seen it, since I'd gotten all my information from Libby. Something was strange, but it took me a minute to figure it out—the phone number.

"Where did you get this?" I asked Mr. Mankewicz.

"The casting lady . . . Pamela something. She was sending them all over town."

555-7716. That was the number Libby gave me. That was the one I had called over and over and over. This flyer said 555-4443.

"Could I ask you a huge favor, Mr. Mankewicz?"

"Probably not," he answered.

"I need to make a phone call. Would you let me use your phone?"

"Local?" he asked.

"Yes."

He handed me his phone and I dialed the number Libby had given me weeks ago. I could feel my heart suddenly pounding like I was nervous about who might pick up. But then, there was that funny tone that happens when you call a disconnected number.

This mailbox is no longer accepting messages. This number is out of service.

I leaned on the counter with the phone still in my hand, trying to figure out if there was any way to know for sure if that number belonged to Libby Chamber.

Had she given me the wrong number from the very start? Did she actually set up a fake message on some random cell phone to throw me off? Was that how she knew exactly when I was informed that there were no more audition spots? Because she was the one leaving the messages? Was there any way to PROVE she'd tricked me again?

"My phone?" Mr. Mankewicz said, breaking me out of my trance. "And your mother is honking her horn."

"Right!" I said. "Thank you, Mr. Mankewicz."

"Um," he said.

I tried to pull myself out of my haze, but I felt totally stunned—was I really so stupid that I let her fool me again? And, once again, in a way that I could never totally prove?

I'll tell you one thing—I'm not telling Tammy or Nana about this one. That would be one huge—no—JUMBO bowl of I TOLD YOU SO!!

12 YEARS 5 MONTHS 1 DAY

Well, I would like to report that I had a crazy fun New Year's Eve, but sadly, it was the first year that Mom and Dad said I could stay up to see the ball drop in Times Square in New York City right by all the Broadway theatres . . . and I fell asleep!

I woke up this morning and didn't even remember it was a brand-new year until I got downstairs and Mom said, "Happy New Year, Lainey!"

"Ugh! I fell asleep, didn't I?"

Chip laughed, and Marty said, "Yup, and let me tell you, it was not easy getting you upstairs!"

"Marty!" Mom said, but it was too late.

"Thanks a lot," I said, and then I sat down and ate too many pancakes.

This is the point when Winter Break gets really boring and I hate to say it, but you just want school to start already. It's New Year's Day and it's the weekend. Everything is just waiting to start up again.

School. Play. Movie. EVERYTHING.

All I can do is keep rehearsing the audition scene. (For Hollywood—not the Fat Lady!)

12 YEARS 5 MONTHS 2 DAYS

OBSERVATION: The circus has LOTS of superstitions—just like the theatre.

1. You must enter the circus ring on the right foot to avoid bad luck.

2. It's good luck to keep a hair from an elephant's tail in your pocket.

3. Once a wardrobe trunk is set down backstage, it is bad luck to move it.

4. Whistling backstage is bad luck. (That one is true in theatre, too.)

5. Never eat peanuts backstage.

6. Bringing a peacock feather into the tent brings bad luck.

CONCLUSION: When people are in situations where they can mess up in a way that could be extremely embarrassing, upsetting, or basically deadly, they get very superstitious about NOT messing up!

12 YEARS
5 MONTHS
3 DAYS

SUDDENLY EVERYBODY WANTS TO BE IN SHOW BUSINESS! YOU KNOW WHAT I SAY TO THAT? GET IN LINE!!!!!!

Just to give you an idea of what it was like at school today . . .

> Lainey? I have to cancel your voice lesson. I've got an audition for a part in the movie!
>
> Mr. C.

> I have three of my Sculpeys done!
>
> Tammy

> The MSBF Club is going to visit the set!
>
> Heidi

> Lainey! Do you know who to talk to about being an extra in the movie?
>
> Mrs. Davies

> My mom actually saw Craig Fortuna and he said, "How are you?"
>
> Lenore

> The movie office is on my dad's FedEx delivery route!
>
> Michaela

> They are going to shoot a scene on my street!
>
> Susan

And then? I got home, just wanting a little peace and quiet, and this is what happened: I opened the back door and stepped into the kitchen. Mom was standing there with this silly grin on her face. The phone was in her hand.

"Mom?" I said.

She turned her head toward me and giggled.

"You've got the phone in your hand, but you're not talking to anyone," I informed her.

"Oh!" she yipped. "I was. I just was!"

"Mom?" I said. "You're acting really weird."

"I just got hired to do all the floral work on the movie! I'm supposed to be 'on set' on Friday because they're doing some kind of dinner scene where there are flowers!"

That's when it was my turn to be the one with the goofy look on my face. "So you're actually working on the movie?" I finally asked.

There was such a weird feeling in my stomach. I mean, it's great. Right? My mom's in show business now. Dream-come-true time. Showbiz family. Someone to help pave the way. So cool.

So why does my stomach hurt?

12 YEARS 5 MONTHS 5 DAYS

Okay. You aren't going to believe this one.

I got home from another ridiculous day at school where EVERYONE was talking about the movie and EVERYONE has something to do with something to do with the movie and EVERYONE thinks that their "something" is cooler than everyone else's "something." And hello? Since when do ANY OF THEM CARE about this stuff?

Anyway, I got home and went directly out to the garage to see if Dad was in a good mood. I needed to ask him to make me the stilts. I want to have plenty of time to practice on them since it's been a while since I first used them at my cousin's.

Anyway, I opened the door to the garage and Dad looked up from his worktable and smiled at me.

Let me repeat that.

Dad stopped working, looked up at me, and smiled.

That made me extremely nervous because that's not just Dad in a good mood, that's a different Dad all together.

"Lainey! Nice to see you!"

Weird and weirder.

"Hi, Dad," I said.

"How was school?"

"Um, good," I said, really not knowing what was up.

"What can I do ya for?"

Okay. Say what? *Do ya for?* Seriously?

"Well, um, I'm auditioning for the school play and the part I want has to be able to do something that could be in a circus act so I was wondering if you could build me a pair of stilts. . . ."

That's when I suddenly focused on what Dad had been working on before I showed up.

"I'm sure I could do that, Lainey, but—"

"Is that a theatre light?" I asked him, pointing to the big black canister on his workbench.

"Film, actually." He smiled. "I got hired today by the production company that's shooting the movie. Your mother mentioned that I can fix anything and they were very excited to meet me. Hired me starting now to be on call to fix whatever might need fixing between now and when they leave town."

"So you're working on the movie, too?" My stomach started hurting again.

"How do you like them apples?" He laughed, and that was about all I could take.

My dad doesn't say things like "them apples." And my dad totally does NOT belong in show business.

I started backing toward the door. I just wanted to be in my room. Alone.

"So when do you need those stilts, Lainey?"

"Ummm—"

"How 'bout I just get them done tonight and then you'll have them," he said.

"That would be great, Dad. Really. Thanks!"

Everybody in my house seems to be getting happier and happier. So why am I feeling worse and worse?

Hope you weren't expecting things to calm down. . . .

We're going to do a tribute to the red carpet for the Spring Concert. We're just going to perform songs that have won Oscars! If we get to work right away, we might be ready to perform some of the songs for the cast and crew of the movie before they leave town!

Mr. C.

My husband and I are going to be in the scene at the bus stop!

Mrs. Davies

The MSBF Club sent a welcome basket to Craig Fortuna and we included special notes from each of us!

Heidi

I am inviting the cast and crew to speak at the school. Not because I'm interested in movie stars, mind you, but because I feel it's a good educational opportunity for the students.

Mrs. Patchuck

My driveway was in one of the scenes they shot yesterday!

Susan

Everybody just calls my dad Al now when he stops by the office. He said he's gonna bring me next time and see if he can get me a part.

Michaela

My Sculpeys are done, Lainey! Will you go with me to deliver them to the production office so they can get to the actors?

Tammy

I've figured it out! It was so obvious! Why didn't I figure this out before? I'm going to direct. That's my passion! And Ms. Belter asked me to student-direct the play. So that's my I M Project! It's perfect! PLUS, I've been reading up on Michael Berkley, the movie director, and he talks a lot about "acting is reacting." I think we should work on that for your audition, Lainey. Oh! And by the way, have you been working on your circus skill? We have a LOT of work to do! Because I don't know if you heard or not, but HEIDI is auditioning for the same part as you are!

Lenore

I just have one question:

HOW IS IT THAT EVERYONE ELSE IS MAKING MORE PROGRESS IN SHOW BUSINESS THAN ME?!

So just in case you're wondering, THAT is why I'm sitting up here in the closet in my room eating an ENTIRE bag of spice drops.

And in case you thought it all wasn't weird enough . . . Dad isn't just Happy Dad now. He actually speaks in movie quotes.

Tonight at dinner? Mom walked into the kitchen with dessert she'd gotten from the downstairs freezer and then Dad all of a sudden started acting like an old-time movie star named Humphrey Bogart from an old movie called *Casablanca*. He looked at Mom and said:

```
Of all the gin joints in all the towns in all
the world, she walks into mine.
```

And Mom giggled. Yup. Giggled. Yikes.

12 YEARS 5 MONTHS 7 DAYS

Hopefully you can hear me. I'm ON SET right now and Mr. Berkley just yelled "ACTION!" which means "DON'T MAKE A SOUND UNTIL YOU HEAR 'CUT'!" So, that's why I'm writing so quietly. You better be reading quietly, too!

But seriously, folks, Chip and I get to be ON SET because they're shooting the dinner scene and Mom is here for the flowers in the shot. There are a couple of different vases around the dining room and Mom has to keep them looking fresh.

This is extremely cool. The only thing that would make it cooler would be if Libby weren't actually *in* the dinner scene. She's sitting at the dining room table with Craig Fortuna and Amy LeBlanc, who play her mom and dad, and Debi Buslik, who plays her aunt. I guess this scene is the last "family dinner" before Craig Fortuna's character gets on the bus and heads to the army base on his way to the Middle East.

I have to say, Libby doesn't look very happy. She actually looks a little nervous. I hope part of the reason she's nervous is because I'm here. That would make me feel better.

"CUT!" Mr. Berkley just yelled. And now everybody's running in every direction. Mom is fluffing flowers. The hair lady is boofing Debi Buslik's hair. The makeup lady is sweeping a brush back and forth over Amy LeBlanc's forehead. Nobody is doing anything to

Libby. She's just slumping in her chair, looking lost. It makes me a teeny bit happy.

There's a lighting guy named Eric who keeps holding up a little meter to check something to do with the light. There's a woman named Heather, who Mom says is the script supervisor and part of her job is making sure things don't change from take to take. For example, making sure the same number of buttons stay buttoned on an actor's sweater throughout a scene because sometimes there are breaks between takes and the actor might take off the sweater and then put it back on. It's her job to make sure the sweater looks just like it did before the break. She's even in charge of making sure every chair, lamp, plant—everything!—is positioned exactly right. So obviously, she keeps checking with Mom since plants get moved around a lot.

"The tulip is drooping, Louise," she just said to Mom. "Can we get a new one or prop that one up?"

"Already on it," Mom said right back, and she turned around and showed Heather a red tulip that was already in her hand.

Mom is so on it. I think she could probably have a full-on career as a Hollywood florist if she wanted one.

Now everyone is just sort of standing around. They're all ready for the next take, but Mr. Berkley is talking to his cameraman and some other guy. He's pointing toward the table and it almost looks like he's pointing at Libby. Maybe she's going to get fired! Maybe they hate her!

OMG! Mr. Berkley is walking toward me—or Mom, actually. But he's definitely walking toward US! brb . . .

Unbelievable!

It's much later now. I really didn't feel like writing after what happened. I don't feel like writing now either, but I know I have a duty to report the truth and only the truth, as it happened—the good, the bad, and the ugly. So, here goes.

First off, I was right about a couple of things. Mr. Berkley was definitely walking toward Mom and he wasn't happy with how the scene looked and it DID have to do with the casting of Craig Fortuna's family.

HOWEVER, that's where my luck ran out. And folks, I mean SERIOUSLY ran out.

Here's what Mr. Berkley said when he got to Mom.

"Mrs. McBride?"

"Yes?" Mom sounded suddenly really nervous.

"I was just wondering if you might consider letting your child be in this scene."

I didn't mean to, but I must have gasped really loud, and I definitely jumped down off the stool I was sitting on because I stepped on Mom's foot.

"Ow!" she squawked.

"Oh!" Mr. Berkley jumped back a little. "Oh, I'm sorry, Lainey. I'm sorry. I was actually referring to your brother."

Everybody's head turned pretty much at the same time to look at Chip, who was so busy reading the manual to his new iPod that it took him a second to realize everyone in the room was staring at him.

"You'd like Chip in the dinner scene?" Mom asked, and I appreciated the fact that she sounded pretty much as shocked as I felt.

"The shot looks imbalanced and I think it would be good to add a boy to the family. And your son looks like he could fit in . . . not to mention, he's got the right energy for this moment."

Mom turned to Chip, who looked about as excited as a worm.

"Would you like to be in the movie, Chip?" Mom asked.

Chip shrugged.

SERIOUSLY?!?! He's living MY DREAM and all he does is SHRUG?!

"Do you think you could play quiet and sad, Chip?" Mr. Berkley asked.

I had to slap my hand on my mouth to keep from laughing. Could he play anything else? That's the real question. Talk about typecasting!

Next thing I knew Mr. Berkley was shouting "ACTION!" and Chip was sitting across from Libby, next to Amy LeBlanc, and looking like he wanted to disappear from that table . . . just like he does every night at home.

I would like to say that's as bad as the day got, but right after Chip got put into wardrobe, Marty showed up. He barely said hello to us before he somehow got himself standing right next to Mr. Berkley. Then he was talking to Mr. Berkley between cuts and Mr. Berkley was introducing him to the cameraman, who handed Marty that little meter thing and showed him whatever it is that it does with the light.

And now? Now, I'm just sitting here in my room, preparing to be told that my family is relocating to Hollywood but they'd like me to stay home to feed the cat.

Am I alone here, people? Or do all of you join me in thinking this whole situation has gotten entirely out of hand!?!?!

12 YEARS
5 MONTHS
8 DAYS

NOTE TO SELF:
FOCUS ON HOLLYWOOD
DIVECCHIO AUDITION.

OR ELSE:
LOSE MY MIND!!!

12 YEARS 5 MONTHS 9 DAYS

Well, we just dropped off all of Tammy's Sculpeys at the production office. There was just one guy there—a PA. He said he would make sure everybody got theirs.

Amy LeBlanc   Debi Buslik   Craig Fortuna

I don't know. I'm not sure it was the best move to just leave the Sculpeys there. But, it's what Tammy wanted to do.

"It's fine, Lainey," she said as we got outside. "Anyway, I'm just glad I did it. It was fun."

"Sometimes you are disturbingly well-adjusted."

"Come on, Lainey." She laughed. "You really have to get back to practicing your stilt walking! Your audition is tomorrow, isn't it?"

"Yes, it is!" I said. "Let's go!"

12 YEARS 5 MONTHS 10 DAYS

True Confession: I'm really glad for Lenore that she's figuring out her passion and has found herself an I M Project, BUT it was really weird to audition for her and I'm not loving the feeling that she knows more about how things are going for my career than I do!

Here's the problem—this audition did not exactly go like I expected. I mean, I read really well, but it turns out Heidi Almighty has decided she's an actress, too.

Yes, you heard me correctly. Heidi Almighty thinks she should be Hollywood DiVecchio and, to make matters worse, Mrs. Belter is taking her seriously!

I mean . . . seriously?

I swear Heidi is just doing this to cause me pain and suffering. When she walked into the auditorium, she looked right at me and smiled. Then she walked up to me and said, "Whattya know, Lainey? We're both auditioning for the same part!" Then, her groupies—um, I mean, friends—Susan and Michaela giggled as they followed Heidi to her seat.

Mrs. Belter started the auditions by thanking everyone for coming.

"We're going to have everybody read at least once and probably more than once and maybe even in parts you really didn't even consider. Please just stay focused and give each reading your very best effort. You never know where you might end up so I want everyone to have the best chance they can have!"

She called up a couple of the boys first. They read for the Strong Man and the Lion Tamer. Then she called my name.

"Lainey? On the stage, please. You'll be reading with"—she looked down at her clipboard—"Heidi."

What are the chances!? Ugh!

That's when things got rocky.

Mrs. Belter handed us both a piece of paper and said, "I know you haven't seen this scene between Hollywood and her mother, but I'd like you to just give it a go. See what happens. Lainey? You read Hollywood first. Heidi, you read the mother. Okay, ladies? When you're ready."

I didn't do so badly for a cold reading, but Mrs. Belter kept saying, "Okay, switch parts, please," and Heidi and I went back and forth being Hollywood and her mom.

I have to say, Lenore sat there with absolutely no expression on her face. I mean, I understand. I do. She's being professional and not playing favorites. But honestly? I started to feel a little bit like she was not being a loyal friend. Couldn't she have slipped me a thumbs-up or something?

Okay.

I haven't actually told you the worst news. After Mrs. Belter was done having me and Heidi switch back and forth, she had me stay up on the stage while other kids came up to read.

And I wasn't up there to read the part of Hollywood.

I was there to read the part of Nel.

The Fat Lady.

12 YEARS 5 MONTHS 11 DAYS

I'm considering putting together a second publication—in addition to my Drama Diaries, I think there might be enough material in my life to write more than one thing at a time. The second one will be called:

The Conflicts of Lainey McBride

With Lenore . . .

"So?" I said when she arrived at the lunch table.

Lenore tilted her head like she had no idea what I was talking about.

All I could think was: *Really? That's how this is going to go?*

"The audition, Lenore," I said in a hushed voice. "What did Mrs. Belter say by the end?"

Lenore looked at me like I had just asked her to give me her iPod—fully loaded—for keeps.

"Sorry," I said. (There might have been just a teeny-weeny bit of sarcasm in it.)

"You want me to jeopardize my integrity as the student-director just to tell you things that aren't even final anyway?"

After that comment, it was me looking at her like she took my iPod—for keeps—but my iPod happens to hold the only pictures I will ever have of my dead dog. Short version? The look I gave her was WAY worse!

"Callbacks are tomorrow," she said to me, and she actually sounded mad. "That's all I have to say."

Well! Smell you! I thought. But I didn't say it. Because that would definitely have had sarcasm in it.

With Mr. C. . . .

"I'm really excited," he said, instead of telling me that my high note on "You're the Top" was pitch-perfect. "I'm going to have a line in the scene I'm in. I just found out yesterday."

"Cool," I said.

There might have been just a teeny-weeny bit of sarcasm in it.

With the World at Large . . .

I went to the set to meet Mom after my voice lesson. I was looking forward to it because today there wouldn't be any Libby. And Chip is over at his friend's house, so I knew he wouldn't be there either. It was just supposed to be me and all the people who are working on the movie.

A much better scenario . . . except it wasn't.

Because Heidi and Michaela and Susan were standing in the middle of the floor when I got there.

And it got worse.

They were being interviewed by WKOK-TV out of Kokomo.

And worse.

They were talking about the Movie Star Boyfriend Club.

"Well," I could hear Heidi Almighty rattling on, "I started the club and it's really caught on at school. These are the founding members, and Michaela's Movie Star Boyfriend has always been Craig Fortuna from the very first day!"

AND WORSE!

"Michaela?" It was a man's voice and I didn't realize at first who was talking but then I saw Craig Fortuna sneaking up behind her . . . WITH A BIG BOUQUET OF FLOWERS!!

On camera.

Close-ups, no doubt.

WKOK-TV actually staged the whole thing for their newscast, because, apparently, the Movie Star Boyfriend Club is newsworthy!

We can just stop here, right? We don't need to go into all the squealing girl-screaming tears of joy that followed?

I wonder sometimes just exactly how long Heidi Almighty will be the bane of my existence.

Because it's already getting old.

Let's see. If it's Wednesday it must be . . . oh, I remember . . . a BAD DAY! Same goes for Tuesday and Thursday and Friday and Monday . . . just in case you're counting.

I think Hollywood coming to me was the wrong move. I think I need to go to Hollywood so that I can actually have a hometown to come home to. Because I gotta tell you, right now, I don't even recognize this place.

I kid you not—there isn't a soul in Fairmount who is not involved in this movie and it's like a contagious disease—like the disease in that movie *The Germ*. No one can outrun it, and once it touches you, you apparently can't help but look for ways to be in show business . . . EVEN IF YOU HAVE NO NATURAL TALENT, INTEREST, OR EXPERIENCE!

One excellent example of that: Heidi is seriously going after MY part in the school play. She even juggled at the callbacks today. Since when does she juggle?

Let me just say this, folks—if I don't get the lead in the school play, it will be like I've gone backward about seventeen thousand steps. It will feel like I've made no progress at all from that day when I was five and I announced that I was going into show business.

It's AT LEAST seventeen thousand steps.

I mean, it's one thing to have to duke it out for a big part at the Kokomo Players and lose out to Libby Chamber, who might actually be headed to Hollywood or Broadway herself. But to think that I might not be able to run the show at Fairmount Elementary School and write my own ticket as to what part I want to play?

Well. That's just pure humiliation.

"Lainey? Would you mind reading Nel once more?"

That was basically all I heard all afternoon. She let me read for Hollywood two different times. I lost track of how many times Heidi read for Hollywood.

Me.

Fat Lady.

I got two words for you:

Worst.

Nightmare.

So after school, I got to go to the set again, which, I have to say, is starting to be not as much fun as I thought it would be.

Mom was doing the flowers for a party scene on the same set where they shot the dinner scene. There were more people in this scene, but it wasn't the really big scene that they asked me to be in. That's happening on Monday.

But, of course, Libby and Chip were both in this one. So I had to stand off to the side and watch Chip be Chip. He just leaned on the fake wall like he was holding it up, and Mr. Berkley kept saying, "Very nice, Chip."

Huh?

That's what you're thinking, right?

Well, I'm with you. Huh?

Libby, on the other hand, kept inching out into the room and Mr. Berkley kept saying, "Stay with Chip, Libby. I want to see a brother-sister moment, watching this grown-up party and feeling like you just want to be with your dad."

> JUST BETWEEN YOU AND ME:
> I don't mind seeing Libby being told she's not doing something right. It gives me a warm and fuzzy feeling right in the middle of my heart. I know. Not nice. You know what? Don't care.

"Lainey!" Suddenly, Tammy was right in front of me.

"What are you doing here?" I asked.

"Quiet on the set!"

Mom spun around and gave Tammy and me a really serious look. So I took Tammy's arm and we walked all the way to the back of the big barn where all the equipment was being stored.

"What are you doing here?" I whispered.

"I tried to call you as soon as I got home," she whispered back. "There was a message on my machine from that Alice lady and she said that the actors got their Sculpey dolls and they wanted to meet me!"

I pulled back to look at Tammy more clearly. She was kind of bouncing up and down, not exactly the way she usually acts.

"So," she continued, "when I got here, one of the PAs was waiting for me and took me right to the makeup trailer. Craig and Amy and Debi were all there! And when I walked in, they cheered! Amy? Amy LeBlanc? She said, 'This is the best present I ever got!'

And Debi? Debi Buslik—"

"I know which Debi!" I snapped, and then I tried to rein in the dark mood that was taking over inside me.

"Right." Tammy didn't even seem to notice my snittiness. "Anyway, she said, 'You have a real artistic talent, Tammy. These are amazing!' And you know what?" Tammy stopped talking for just a second, but I wasn't fast enough to get in a response before she started talking again. "They each had their Sculpley standing on their makeup tables! And then the makeup lady asked me how much I charge because she would love to give some as presents!"

Finally, she stopped talking.

But I didn't know what to say.

"Isn't that amazing?" she asked, forgetting to whisper.

"Shh!" I said.

"Well, isn't it?" she whispered.

"Truly!" I said. "What did Craig Fortuna say?"

Tammy giggled.

"What?" I asked.

"He just kind of put out his arms like I was supposed to walk up to him and then he hugged me and kissed me on the cheek!"

"Wow," I said.

And honestly—that was all I could figure to say. Tammy is now, like, everyone's new best friend, PLUS she's about to become a paid professional.

"So are you going to make more Sculpeys for the makeup lady?"

"Oh, I don't know. I'm not sure she really meant that. She was just being nice. But she did say if I wanted to get my makeup done, I could come back when she wasn't busy and she'd give me a real Hollywood makeover."

STOP!

I just have to stop.

I want to be happy for everyone. Really. I do. My mom. My dad. Marty. Chip. Tammy. Lenore.

But that is NOT the emotion I'm feeling.

If I were Tammy—you know, gracious, kind, and generous Tammy? That would be the emotion I'd be feeling. But I'm not. I'm Lainey.

Lainey Mc-I-Hate-Feeling-Invisible.

12 YEARS 5 MONTHS 13 DAYS

```
The Place: Cafeteria, Fairmount Elementary
The Time: Lunch
The Action: CLIMB Meeting
The Players: Me, Tammy, Lenore, Heidi
The Feeling: Utterly utter utterness . . .


                    LENORE
It's an utter disaster! Mrs. Belter was rushed
to the hospital last night. Appendicitis!


                    TAMMY
Oh, no! Is she okay?


                    LAINEY
Did she finish casting?
```

Lenore's and Tammy's heads turned in utter unison. They just stared at me with a look of utter disgust and I knew. Me. In the doghouse. That was utterly the wrong response. I knew it as soon as I said it—that I should be more concerned about Mrs. Belter than the play . . . but SERIOUSLY! What about the casting?

```
                    LENORE
She was in utter agony last night, I guess,
but now that she's had the surgery, she's just
groggy and can't really move around much.
```

                    TAMMY
Should we send her something? I could make her
a Sculpey!

I let my head fall forward a little bit so that I was looking down
when my eyes rolled. I knew it was going to be utterly impossible
to keep myself from rolling my eyes so at least I kept anyone from
seeing it. I mean, I don't want to say the Sculpey thing is getting
old, but hasn't she gotten enough Sculpey attention for one week?

                    LENORE
I have to write a notice for the bulletin
board saying there's going to be a delay in
announcing the cast and I'm supposed to get
all her notes from her desk and leave them in
the front office for her husband to pick up and
bring to her and—

                    LAINEY
Her notes?

Yeah, I knew I'd get the looks. I didn't care.

                    LAINEY
Seriously. Her notes on the auditions? Do you
know what her decision is, Lenore? Did I get
Hollywood? Do you actually know the answer to
that question and aren't telling me even now
that we're going to have to wait FOREVER to find
out from Mrs. Belter?

                    LENORE
Lainey! Stop putting me in an utterly impossible position. I am not going to gossip about
the play. It's too important for that.

                    LAINEY
    So you are actually standing there and telling
    me that you aren't going to tell me anything
    more than you tell . . . Heidi, for example?

I looked at Tammy, but then looked away from her. She was clearly in agreement with Lenore. Then, out of the blue—some might call it an utter miracle—Heidi walked up to our table.

                    HEIDI
    I just heard about Mrs. Belter. Is she okay?

                    LENORE
    She's going to be fine, but the casting
    announcement for the play is going to be
    delayed. I'll be posting a notice later today.

                    HEIDI
    I'm glad she's doing okay.

Lenore smiled at Heidi. Then, she glanced quickly in my direction with a look that very clearly said:

That is the proper response to this situation.

So I replied with a look that very clearly said:

Utter Betrayal!

I am not even going to comment on the situation. I will just report the events. That's what I am supposed to be doing anyway. I'm archiving my journey to stardom so that the biographies and movies and retrospectives will be accurate. And trust me, if they are accurate, this will not be one of the "happy montage" moments.

No . . . these last few weeks? They will be shot in low light with music in a minor key and when it is over, the audience will be completely stunned by the determination and strength of Lainey McBride. Because *nobody* should have to endure *EVERYBODY* in their (her) life getting a better shot at fame and immortality than them (her).

But as I said, I'm not even going to comment. I'll just tell you the story of today.

> Once upon a time, there was a nana who made monthly visits to see her family in Fairmount, Indiana. The family, especially the young girl in the family, was always excited for the visit. But one day, the town of Fairmount got taken over by a big glamorous Hollywood movie, and everything changed.
>
> This time, when the nana visited the family, her son was working with the crew of the movie, her daughter-in-law was making flower arrangements for

the movie, her oldest grandson was assisting the lighting director, and her youngest grandson (a slender boy with a gift for turning invisible whenever there was trouble) had suddenly become the local star of the movie.

Of course, the nana's favorite person in the family, her beloved granddaughter, named Lainey, had yet to be given the opportunity to shine in the movie. And the nana KNEW that all Lainey had ever wanted was to be an actress of the highest order. AND she knew how hurt and upset Lainey had become over the way things had been going with the big glamorous movie.

So when Lainey got to the set after school to visit her mom, the last thing Lainey expected was to see the nana IN THE MIDDLE OF THE SCENE AT THE NURSING HOME WHERE CRAIG FORTUNA IS SAYING GOODBYE TO HIS MOTHER BEFORE GOING OFF TO WAR. THE LAST THING LAINEY EXPECTED WAS THAT THE NANA WOULD GET CAST AS CRAIG FORTUNA'S MOTHER'S ROOMMATE AND THAT THE NANA WOULD HAVE LINES TO SAY RIGHT TO CRAIG FORTUNA!!!!

THE NANA AS ROOMMATE
Don't you worry, honey.

The nana is lying in the bed next to the bed where the actress who is playing the mother of Craig Fortuna is lying. The nana is wearing a nightie for a costume and has some makeup on and is glowing under the big Hollywood lights. The camera is about four feet away from her face.

THE NANA AS ROOMMATE
We're gonna take care of your momma until you come home again, safe and sound.

Craig Fortuna is staring at the nana as he nods and a tear rolls down his face.

Then the director yells, "CUT!"

And everyone applauds.

Yes. I'll repeat that for those of you who might not have been paying attention as carefully as you should have been, or perhaps were just too shocked to really take it in.

The crew all gathered around the nana and applauded because she was so good in the scene, which apparently she had somehow JUST been cast in because the lady who was supposed to be in the other bed had developed some kind of bronchitis. The nana had come with her daughter-in-law that morning to "take a look-see at all the excitement" and suddenly the nana was "discovered" and on her way to being a movie star.

And everyone—except Lainey—lived happily ever after.

The End

"Well, it was the darndest thing"—Nana laughed as she passed the salad to Marty—"I was just standing there helping your mother freshen up an arrangement and all of a sudden people were asking me if I would like to be in a movie!"

"Do you think we'll end up in any scenes together, Nana?" Chip asked. He was looking up and smiling. Then he took a big gulp of milk just so he could look even more perfectly perfect as "The Kid in the Happy Family."

"Oh, I don't think so, sweetie." She laughed.

"No," Marty said between bites. "I was looking at the shooting schedule when Michael and Stu were talking through the shot today. There aren't any more scenes in the house or in the nursing home."

"I'm still swamped with work though." Mom laughed. "But now it's doing arrangements for different crew members and what have you. Reba, the makeup lady? She ordered half a dozen arrangements for Fairmount folks who have helped her while she's here! And that's only the top of the pile!"

"Don't you just love Reba?" Nana said as she leaned forward with wide eyes, talking to everyone at the table.

"She was really nice to me." Chip nodded.

"What else did you see on the shooting schedule, Marty?" Dad asked as he cut a piece of pork on his plate.

"Well, the big crowd scene is Monday," he said. "Then it looks like the rest of the week is going to be at the hardware store."

"Oh, sure!" Dad nodded, pointing at Marty with his knife. "That's right. That's where they want me on set for most of the week. Been so busy repairing the cable and lights, I clean forgot!"

Mom laughed and Marty smiled while he nodded and shoved an entire roll in his mouth.

"I think it's so interesting the way Mr. Berkley works with the actors, don't you, Lainey?" Nana asked.

My whole body jerked because I was so startled to hear my name. I don't usually hear the characters in the TV shows that I'm watching say my name. They don't usually talk directly to me.

But this is a new show. I've never seen it before. It's called *Happy Family*. Personally, I don't think it's going to make it. It's pretty freaky and totally confusing. I'm betting it gets canceled. It's just not believable.

"Lainey?" Nana asked again.

I turned toward her and stared right into her face. Then I looked from face to face until I'd studied every person at the table. It's soooo weird. They look so much like my real family.

12 YEARS 5 MONTHS 16 DAYS

"I'm telling you, it's like they've all been possessed. Everyone was talking to each other and nodding and laughing."

I was talking to Lenore, who came over to hang out even though things have been a little tense between us with the whole "she knows more than I do about my career" business.

"It sounds nice, if you ask me," she said, not looking up from her book.

I was looking at the most recent issue of *People*, the one with Redmond Roberts on the cover. (I have to be especially gentle with it since Redmond is the love of Tammy's life and this is her copy that she's planning to save forever!)

Lenore was flipping through a book on set design. ("A director needs to be able to contribute to all aspects of a production," she'd informed me when she walked into my room today with the book.)

She is really taking this directing business seriously. I mean, it's good. I'm impressed. It just seems like, all of a sudden, she's an expert on everything theatrical.

"I guess it would be nice," I agreed with her, "if it wasn't because they've all decided they're in show business and know as much about it as some of us who have been committed to the profession for a long, long time."

"Why don't you just be happy that your family is having a good time with all this?"

"Because," I snapped, "they don't belong in show business and I do!"

I could tell that probably didn't sound very good, but it's what it feels like. At least I'm honest.

"Well," she said, and she glanced up at me with a look in her eyes that made my stomach feel tense, "you might just consider that you should be grateful you have a family that's all together. About anything!"

That's when I felt the slam of serious guilt. I should have realized that Lenore would feel that way. Her family is pretty much a mess, or at least that's how it seems. Her mom is always working at a job that embarrasses Lenore and I get the feeling she's had a bunch of boyfriends that Lenore hasn't really liked. And her dad? Well, I don't even know if Lenore knows where he is.

I was about to apologize and try to explain how I was feeling in a different way that wouldn't make Lenore feel even worse about her life. But then she said, "You don't *own* theatre, Lainey. Just because you're the one who is always talking about it, doesn't mean you know the most about everything!"

"Well, you don't know everything either!" I said.

"You should be glad there are other people interested and involved." Lenore stood up and grabbed her coat. "If there weren't, there wouldn't be a business to be in!"

"I didn't say I didn't want other people involved. I just said my family has never been artistic until all of a sudden—now it's all they talk about! That's all!"

"Ever since I met you, all you complained about was how they didn't understand you because you're an artist. So how come you're still complaining now that you all have something in common?!"

She was pretty much shouting as she stood in the doorway of my room.

"Well, if you would just tell me what's going on with the school play, I might be in a better mood!" I shouted back.

"What?!" Lenore snapped. "What does that have to do with what we're talking about?"

"Because!" I said, since I really couldn't explain what it had to do with it even though it seemed totally certain that it did. So then I just said it again, "Because!"

"I'm going home!" Lenore announced.

Like it was supposed to be a big surprise.

12 YEARS 5 MONTHS 17 DAYS

Even though:

- Lenore was TOTALLY mean to me yesterday and left in a huff
- I don't have a real part and I'm only an extra
- Libby and Chip are both really close to the camera in this scene
- Marty is actually sitting in a director's chair by the camera
- EVERYONE has bigger jobs than me on the movie
- We're shooting outside at the very unglamorous bus depot
- AND IT'S ONLY 9 DEGREES

I cannot tell a lie—this is really, really fun!

I just love being in the scene with everything happening all around me. It's like being inside a bubble world, and outside the bubble there are a dozen people fixing and finishing and adjusting things that are inside the bubble world, but they don't really come into it. They stand outside it and watch. Only the most special people live inside the bubble, and today I am one of them.

I'm writing this right now between takes. It's kind of tricky since it's too cold to take my gloves off and it's hard to hold this notebook while I'm standing up because we're not supposed to move from where Mr. Berkley has positioned us. But I don't want to risk missing anything so I'm writing as much as I possibly can.

It's 9:30 A.M. and we've been here since 7:00 A.M. We're shooting the scene where the character that I SHOULD BE PLAYING, BUT LIBBY IS PLAYING INSTEAD has her line. All the extras in the scene (there are fifteen of us) are standing alongside a Greyhound bus. Craig Fortuna is standing with Amy LeBlanc, Debi Buslik, Libby, and Chip by the door of the bus. The action of the scene is that he's hugging everybody good-bye. The last person he says good-bye to is MY CHARACTER THAT LIBBY IS PLAYING. That's when he says, "It'll be better when I'm gone, sweetheart. You'll see." And then MY CHARACTER THAT LIBBY IS PLAYING says the big line.

We (the extras) are supposed to start saying good-bye and waving as soon as Craig Fortuna turns away from his family and gets on the bus. The scene doesn't end until the bus actually starts to pull away.

We've done it four times now and I'm not really sure why Mr. Berkley isn't happy with the shot. But it's okay with me because I definitely don't want to go back to school today and the longer I get to be in the bubble the better! I've been trying to catch Marty's eye because he might be able to tell me what's going on. But apparently he's too busy sitting in the director's chair and being important to notice me staring at him.

I must say, the good thing about Chip is that he hasn't really changed even though he has ended up being one of the biggest Fairmount stars in the movie. I guess it's because he doesn't really care. It's like he's doing it because he has to—like math or something. He's totally weird, but at least he's not stuck-up. Not like Libby, who hasn't said much to me since the shooting started even though she does still give me little waves like we're best friends.

What's she thinking? Does she believe those little waves are enough to keep me believing we're friends? Like that will be enough to make me trust her again when she needs to trick me out of another chance for my big break in showbiz? Because it's pretty clear that she tried to keep me from auditioning for this movie. I mean I can't exactly prove it, but it's what Nana and Tammy think. No doubt.

Hold on a minute.

Mr. Berkley just pulled Libby away from the other actors. I have to say she doesn't look very good. She's totally shivering and her lips are blue.

Hold on, I'm going to try to listen to what he's saying. . . .

!!!!!!!!

Okay, you aren't going to believe this! Guess why we keep reshooting this scene! Just guess!

OK, TIME'S UP:

BECAUSE LIBBY CAN'T STOP SHAKING!

I just eavesdropped on Mr. Berkley talking to her. This is what he said:

"Libby, do you think if you went inside and warmed up you'd be able to do a take without the shivering? I understand it's cold, but you're shivering so much it's making it hard to understand what you're saying."

I'll be honest with you, I would tell you what Libby said back to him but—I COULDN'T REALLY UNDERSTAND HER! Ha!

So now we're all on a break because of Delicate Little Libby. I mean, I'm cold, too, but you don't see me shivering!

MAYBE IF LIBBY GAINED A LITTLE BODY FAT SHE MIGHT BE ABLE TO SURVIVE OUTDOORS FOR MORE THAN THIRTY SECONDS! I wonder if Mr. Berkley has real-ized yet that if he'd cast me instead of the Starving LITTLE Waif, he'd be done with this shot and moving on to the next setup! My BIGness would have gotten the job done!

Hold on . . . something else is happening. Mr. Berkley is looking over here. I think he's actually looking at me. He's got his arm raised up and he keeps waving it across the scene. He points from where Craig Fortuna stands, across the parking lot of the bus depot, and then stops when he gets to me.

Maybe they're deciding to replace Libby with me.

MAYBE MY BODY FAT WILL ACTUALLY GET ME CAST!!

"Is she warmed up?" Mr. Berkley asks one of the assistants.

The assistant heads up to the trailer where Libby has been warming up her Delicate LITTLE Self.

I have to say, Mr. Berkley doesn't look like he's having a very good time. The smile he gives Libby when she comes back to her spot isn't exactly believable.

"Better?" he asks Libby.

"Yes." She smiles. "Sorry."

I know I'm supposed to be looking at Craig Fortuna when Mr. Berkley shouts "ACTION!" but I can't help it, I'm staring at Libby. It doesn't even take thirty seconds before she's vibrating again.

"CUT!" Mr. Berkley yells. "Can we get some more blankets here?" he shouts, and he points at Libby. Then he and his cameraman walk away from all the actors. They're whispering about something. They turn their backs so I can't see their faces.

ARGH! I cannot hear them even though they are just about ten feet away. I'm pretending not to look at them because if they turn around and look for me, I don't want to look too desperate. Because maybe they're deciding to replace Libby?! AND, maybe they're trying to replace Libby with me?!

"Too bad the other one's in the can," the cameraman says when they finally turn back.

"It's fine," Mr. Berkley says, "this will work."

Then he turns to us and says, "We're going to shoot this once more and I'm sure we're going to get it this time. Thank you so much for your patience and please remember, do NOT look at the camera EVER!"

He's walking back to the camera.

Okay. Well. So much for me getting the part, I guess.

I don't get it. It doesn't look like they're changing anything. It doesn't make sense. I can see Libby shaking from here. How can Mr. Berkley be so sure he'll get his shot when Libby is still a jiggly mess?

"Okay, people, let's make this the one!"

Forget it. It doesn't matter. I don't want to feel bad today. I'm over getting that part anyway. I was having a great time before I thought they were going to recast it so I'm going to go back to that! I'm going to be an Extraordinary Extra!

"ACTION!"

I do just like Mr. Berkley says. I NEVER look at the camera. In fact, I decide not even to look at Libby. I look at Craig Fortuna and you know what? He's a really good actor. I was just watching him say good-bye to everyone and he seemed so hurt, like he was so sorry about all the things he'd done wrong, it made me feel like crying.

"CUT!" Mr. Berkley shouted. "Great! That's it, everyone! I think we have it!"

I swear Libby is still completely vibrating. I really don't understand how they can think that take was any different. But everyone is clapping so obviously—IT'S A WRAP!—as they say in Hollywood.

I wish it wasn't.

I just realized what the cameraman meant when he said "the other one's in the can." He was talking about other scenes that were already shot. That's what "in the can" means—that the scene is shot and done.

That's probably the reason they didn't replace Libby with me. They couldn't put me in the scene today no matter what Libby did because they'd already shot the other scenes with her character, so they had to stay with her no matter how hopeless she was. Ugh! I swear I almost had that part . . . again.

12 YEARS 5 MONTHS 18 DAYS

FROM: StarChamber@yippee.com
TO: LaLaLainey@yippee.com

SUBJECT: Wanted to let you know . . .

Lainey!

The Diary of Anne Frank opens tomorrow night and I REEEEE-
AAAAAALLLLY hope you'll come. I got four tickets for you so
you can bring your family. They are at the box office. All you
have to do is show up. Will you? I hope so!!

xxoo,

Libby

P.S. How about that cold yesterday? That was crazy! Sorry I
haven't been able to talk to you much lately, but I just didn't
want Mr. Berkley to think I wasn't professional . . . you get it,
right?

Well, what do you know? I guess Libby figures it is still worth
her while to keep me fooled. Here's the thing: If Libby didn't think
I was a real threat to her career—if she didn't feel like my talent
might be bigger than her talent—then she wouldn't work so hard
at destroying me. So I feel like it's kind of a compliment.

That might be a little twisted, but it's also very showbizzy. I've
read about these kinds of situations between lots of actresses who

are always going for the same parts.

This is what Tammy said when I showed her the email:

"I knew she was going to do something like this. And I know you're going to go, Lainey. You are soooo weird about Libby Chamber."

"I have to go, Tam. Opening Nights are a big deal. Libby is not the only one who can use people, you know. I can *use* Libby. Who knows? Maybe I'll see Rodney Vaccaro and he'll offer me a part in something. Or maybe I'll see some of the movie people. They might be there, you know."

"Don't you think it's going to be hard to watch her do that part?"

"It'll be worse to sit home and just know it's going on."

Tammy stared at me—for a really long time—with her hands on her hips. I'm not sure what she was trying to do—maybe put a spell on me so I would turn into a statue until tomorrow is over or something. Finally, she spoke.

"You are not allowed to go unless you go with me."

"Okay," I said. "If that's how you want to do it. But you can't say anything mean to Libby. I am handling her in my own way and it's better if she doesn't think I know what a snake she is."

Tammy stared at me awhile again. "Fine," she said at last. "But you might want to think about spending as much energy on making up with Lenore as you do on figuring out how to handle Libby Chamber—because unlike Libby, Lenore is actually your friend."

"Don't be so sure," I said.

"I am sure," she said, and then she dropped the subject. "So anyway, I've already talked to Todd, because I knew this was going to come up, and he said he would drive us tomorrow. So, be ready at seven. Talk to you later."

She turned away and headed down the hall toward science class. I just stood there staring at her from behind and all I could think was this: CLIMB must really be working because that girl is turning into a real force of nature . . . as Nana would say.

12 YEARS 5 MONTHS 19 DAYS

Ugh. Really don't feel like writing. I'm a little depressed. Maybe Tammy was right—it wasn't so easy watching Libby be Anne Frank.

Here are the facts: I went. I saw. I came home. I did not see Rodney Vaccaro or Michael Berkley or Pamela Chassin or ANYONE who knows I'm Lainey McBride and not just another person sitting in a seat staring at the star . . . meaning Libby.

Yes. Libby was the star. Yes, her picture was on the cover of the playbill. Yes, she looked amazing.

PLAYBILL
the DIARY of ANNE FRANK

What the playbill would have looked like if I got the part.

She was the center of every scene. Her voice was really strong. She laughed real laughs and cried real tears. The applause at the end was an actual roar and Libby got the last bow. Then the audience stood up and Libby got another bow.

All by herself.

Alone.

In the spotlight.

12 YEARS 5 MONTHS 20 DAYS

"Aren't you going to call us to order?" Tammy asked me after she and Lenore sat down at the lunch table.

I didn't really feel like having a CLIMB meeting. In fact, I didn't even feel like sitting with Tammy and Lenore. I mean, Lenore basically said I was a terrible person and Tammy basically said I was stupid for doing the things I do. But they both stared at me and wouldn't go away, so I didn't have much choice.

"I call this meeting to order," I finally said, but not very loudly.

"Well, I just want to say that I really think CLIMB is helping me!" Tammy smiled at me. "It's amazing how much people like my Sculpeys. It has totally made me feel more confident!"

"That's great, Tam!" Lenore smiled at Tammy like they're best friends.

"So, thanks, Lainey. This was all your idea and it's so cool!"

"You thought of the name." I was trying to hide my real feelings.

"But really, Lainey, it wouldn't exist if it weren't for you!" she insisted.

"Well, if you're so grateful then why did you cheer so loudly for Libby last night!?"

So much for hiding my true thoughts. Honestly, I tried not to say it, but once it started coming out of my mouth, there was no stopping it.

I have to say, I even impress myself with my natural talent for bringing a conversation to a total screeching halt.

Tammy and Lenore both stared at me with totally shocked looks on their faces.

"Tammy just gave you a really nice compliment, Lainey," Lenore said, and there was a sound in her voice that made it clear she was totally disgusted with me.

"You're the one who wanted to go to that stupid show," Tammy said. "I didn't want you to go. Remember? But you insisted and I didn't want you to go alone. Can I help it if it turned out to be a good play?"

"But did you have to cheer so loudly for Libby?"

"She was really good, Lainey!" Tammy shouted.

Did you get that, people?

TAMMY JUST SHOUTED!

And she shouted something extremely mean. She said Libby was really good in the part that I should have been playing. Then she tilted her head a little bit to the side. "I was just about to invite you to get your makeup done with me before the big wrap party tomorrow," she said. She seemed truly stunned, but she kept talking. "Reba said if I made her a Sculpey, she would do my makeup and one of my friends', too. I was just about to ask you if you wanted to show up at the big movie party looking totally glamorous!"

"Don't even bother, Tammy." Lenore stood up from the table. "Lainey doesn't think anyone should be in show business except her." She picked up her lunch tray. "I am going to find another table."

And she walked away. She actually walked away. And then, you know what happened next? Tammy stood up, took her tray, AND FOLLOWED HER!

So now I'm sitting in a stall in the girls' room and all I can think is, I haven't been here in a while. I'm remembering when I used to spend every lunch in the girls' room, back when I first met Lenore. I thought those days were over. How did I end up back here?

FROM: LaLaLainey@yippee.com
TO: SculpeyGirl@yippee.com, SmartArt@yippee.com

SUBJECT: Really Sorry

I'm really sorry. I know that's not a very good apology, but since I don't really know how I got here, it's hard to know what I should apologize for doing. I don't mean to sound like I don't mean that I'm sorry, because I am. Obviously, if everyone is mad at me, there's something I'm doing that's pretty annoying. I mean, I'm not an idiot. I do get that much. I just don't know exactly what it is that I'm doing. But I am sorry for it. You guys are my best friends and I don't want to be in a big fight with you. So if you would just accept my apology for now and when it becomes clear what I'm apologizing for, then I'll re-apologize more specifically. Okay? Please?

Lainey

12 YEARS 5 MONTHS 22 DAYS

Okay. I can't write much because I am in the middle of the

COOLEST

party I have ever been to in my entire life, but I have to make a few notes so that nothing gets lost to history!

First of all, I look

FABULOUS!

Tammy, in Tammy fashion, did not actually respond to my email. She just called this morning and said, "We have to be at the makeups trailer at four P.M. exactly and Reba will do both our make-ups for the party!"

Just like that. No mention of the terrible Lunchtime Fight. No mention of my nonspecific apology email. Just directions on where to be and an email with a picture of the Sculpey she made of Reba.

Reba

So, we got to the trailer and Reba went to work on Tammy first. She showed her which shades of base and blush look best with her skin. She showed her how to cover up a couple of unfortunate zits that flared up on the tip of her nose. She made her eyes look like glimmering jewels. Then she did this swoop-up thing with Tammy's hair and I SWEAR she was a movie star. One swoop and the girl was

101% Tinseltown!

So, then, Reba said, "Okay, Lainey, hop up!"
Well, I don't have to tell you how

EXTRAORDINARY

it was to be sitting in a movie makeup trailer, on a white cushy chair, looking in one of those mirrors with lightbulbs all around it

(AMAZING!)

and hear a real-life Hollywood makeup person say,

"Wow, Lainey, you have stunning skin."

To tell you the truth, I'm surprised she had enough makeup to cover my whole face, because it must have been pretty big, as huge as my head was feeling after that comment.

I HAVE STUNNING SKIN.

When she got to my hair, she said, "These waves are to die for!" I just sort of laughed and shrugged.

"Beautiful!" she said, and then she took two combs and pulled it up from the sides so that I looked like a movie star from like 1940 or something.

Okay, now we're at the party. It's in the barn that's been the soundstage for the last few weeks except now it's like a fancy Beverly Hills restaurant or something. It's all lit up with spotlights and Mom did some amazing, huge flower arrangements that sit all along the sides of the barn in big floor vases. There's excellent music cranked up and people are dancing—I even saw Amy LeBlanc ask Chip to dance! Ha! He looked like he was just praying his spaceship would show up at that very second and take him back to his planet.

And the food? I don't know how all of Hollywood is so skinny if this is how they eat at their parties! There are four really long tables covered in fancy cheese and cracker platters and shrimp platters and little fingery-food-stuff platters.

There are about 4,013,849,623 calories in this barn and I'm not going to eat any of them! I'm toooo excited to eat.

I told you it was important that I sneak off in a corner and write some of this stuff down, because, otherwise, really amazing, once-in-a-lifetime moments might get lost forever. And there you are. We just witnessed one.

I'm actually not hungry.

Make a big check mark by that one, biographers. You'll want to make sure that goes in your books.

Hold on, Tammy is walking up to me.

Okay. She said we have to call Lenore.

"She won't want to come," I said. "She's really mad at me."

Tammy put her hands on her hips and looked me right in the eye. "Seriously?" she said. "Do you really think *you* are what she's going to notice when she walks into this place?" Tammy threw her arms up in the air. "Look around you, Lainey! This party is a way bigger deal than any fight you might have had. This party is the news flash, not you!"

"Ouch," I said, and we both smiled just enough to be sure neither of us had just gotten mad. "Call her," I added.

Because Tammy's right. Lenore shouldn't miss this. As a future award-winning director, she needs to be here!

I'm home.

I'm in bed, but I won't be falling asleep anytime soon, that's for certain. Not with everything that just happened. It's hard to even know where to begin.

This was the most amazing night of my life.

I think I just have to write it like it's happening right now, otherwise I'm afraid I might not be able to make it clear to you just how INCREDIBLE it was . . . the way everything happened.

Okay. Here goes.

About half an hour after we call Lenore, she shows up wearing this incredible outfit that is so many different kinds of black that it's sort of unbelievable. I don't think I realized black came in so many shades. She's wearing leggings and high boots, a skirt that has about seventy-three layers, a blouse with a T-shirt under it, and a jacket that scoops down in the back. Her long black braid is all twisted up behind her head.

"Crikey!" She laughs when she finds us. "You guys weren't kidding! This is amazing!" Then she looks at both of us for a long second and says, "Wow! And you guys look amazing, too!"

"I'm really sorry!" I blurt out. I didn't plan it, but when I saw her I just wanted everything to be okay between us.

"Me too," she says right into my ear so she's sure I hear it over the thumping music and then she hugs me.

Lenore isn't exactly a hugger, so it's pretty shocking.

"You are the best friend I've ever had," she whispers, and that is even more shocking. Plus, it's hard to know what to say back to her because my other best friend is standing right here. It feels great, on one hand, to know I mean so much to Lenore. But on the other hand, I feel really guilty, even though I'm still not so sure what I did.

Luckily, before I can say anything back to her, I realize Debi Buslik and Amy LeBlanc are standing right next to us. Tammy and Lenore see them at the same time and we all kind of gasp. Debi and Amy both turn and look at us and all of us—all five of us—just laugh!

"I can't believe it's you!" Debi Buslik says, teasing us a little bit like she's as amazed to see us as we are to see her!

"I can't believe it's you either!" I say back to her. It's pretty funny.

"You girls look stunning this evening!" Amy says. "Looks like somebody took Reba up on her offer for a makeup session."

Tammy nods. "I made her a Sculpey and she did our makeup in exchange."

"Nice!" Debi says, and she gives Tammy a high five.

"Lenore's a director," I say to them, not wanting her to feel left out since she didn't have amazing makeup. "Very behind-the-scenes, so she doesn't wear makeup!"

Lenore nudges me, like she wants me to shut up now, but she's smiling really big as Debi and Amy introduce themselves and compliment her on her outrageous fashion sense.

"I've been looking for you, Lainey!" I turn around and there's Libby. No surprise she shows up just when we're hanging out with the stars of the movie.

"Hi, Debi," she says like they're best friends. "Hi, Amy!"

"Ladies and gentlemen!"

Mr. Berkley is standing in front of a big screen that just got pulled down on the far wall of the barn. He's holding a microphone and trying to get everyone's attention.

"Fairmount! You are a great town!"

The barn feels like it might fall down with the rumble of screams and cheers that explode all around me.

"We are so sad to be leaving because we've just had a great time," Mr. Berkley goes on, "but now we have to get ready to head to the Middle East, where we're going to shoot the rest of the movie."

There's an excited buzz. Nobody's saying a word, but it just feels like you can reach out and touch pure energy in the air.

"Since it's going to be a while before the movie is actually finished, we didn't want to make you all wait that long to get a sense of what Fairmount is going to look like on the big screen!"

There's another big explosion of cheering.

"I want to thank my amazing crew and some very dedicated editors back in LA who really bent over backward to put together these rough cuts so that you all could see them tonight. Can we take the lights out?" he says to somebody somewhere who's in charge of the lights.

Everything goes dark and I think I might just explode from the excitement.

There's a flicker on the screen and all of a sudden I'm looking at the dinner table scene they shot the day Mr. Berkley asked Chip to be in the movie and there's barely a shot in the whole scene that doesn't have Chip somewhere in it. In fact, his face shows up more than Libby's does, which I try not to notice on purpose, but it just becomes too obvious to ignore. This is when I remember that Libby is standing right beside me. I don't dare even look at her because I'm guessing she's noticed that Chip got more screen time than her, too.

The next scene is outside and whattya know, there's Susan's driveway and there's a bus stop that doesn't actually exist in front of Susan's house and Mrs. Davies and her husband are sitting on the bench!

There are lots of muffled screams because everyone is recognizing a person or a place or whatever. It's hard not to make noise.

Now the party scene is playing and I recognize Mr. C. and Mrs. Patchuck. (Who knew?!) Ms. Erica the librarian from the Fairmount Library got in there, too. I want the images to go by slower so I can study everyone in the background because I probably know half of them. But I guess I'll have to wait on that until the DVD comes out.

Libby makes a little noise and I suddenly realize the party scene just ended and there was no sign of her or Chip. Now I KNOW

I can't look at her. She's probably shooting daggers with her eyes she's so mad. Two of her three scenes have already gone by and she's shown up, but there hasn't really been a "moment" for her.

Nana! WOW! Nana's scene in the nursing home makes the whole place go absolutely silent because it just grabs you the way Craig Fortuna looks at his mom and how he cries that one tear when Nana says her line:

```
We're gonna take care of your momma until you
come home again, safe and sound.
```

It was an Oscar moment. No doubt!

Dad? Dad got himself in the movie? I'm looking at the hardware store on Main Street where they were shooting all this week and Dad is in the background in most all of it! He never said anything at home! He never even mentioned that he was in front of the camera. He looks pretty great, I have to say.

I actually feel Libby's arm tense up when the bus flashes onto the screen. This is the big scene. The good-bye scene. It starts with a long shot of the bus and the whole crowd and I CAN SEE THE BACK OF MY HEAD! AHHH!

Then the camera moves in on the family as they all say their good-byes. Libby grabs my arm as the camera gets to her face and she opens her mouth to start her line, but before she even says a word, the camera slides off her face and pulls out to look at the whole crowd. Libby is still talking, but you don't see her on camera. You see the crowd and the bus stop and then you see just the crowd and then you see part of the crowd and then?

Then?

Then you see me. Just me. You see Lainey McBride, a girl in the crowd, as she watches Craig Fortuna say good-bye to his family. And you see me for A LONG TIME . . . for the whole rest of the speech until at the end? A single tear falls down my cheek and then the camera pulls back and Craig turns away from Libby and climbs onto the bus.

I feel numb. My head is buzzing. I can see Tammy and Lenore jumping up and down in front of me and I can feel Libby's hand release from my arm and actually kind of push me away as she disappears into the crowd. But it all feels like it's at a distance. The screen goes dark and the lights come back up in the room.

"You got the biggest close-up I've ever seen!" Tammy is squealing.

"How did you cry like that?" Lenore asks in amazement. "What technique did you use?"

"I just watched the scene," I say to Lenore as I'm starting to feel like I'm returning to earth.

"You were in the moment." She nods. "See? It really works!"

"You got the longest close-up of anyone in Fairmount!" Tammy half-whispered. "Did you see how Libby stomped off?"

I just laugh. I didn't actually see Libby or anyone else, for that matter. All I'm seeing is signs.

I GOT A CLOSE-UP!

I CRIED REAL TEARS IN A HOLLYWOOD MOVIE!

BODY FAT SAVED THE DAY!

"You look good up there, Lainey."

I turn to see who's talking to me.

"Dad!" I say, and I actually hug him and it almost doesn't feel weird. "So do you!"

"You've got a good face," he says, and he smiles at me like I don't ever remember him doing before.

"Thanks," I say. And I believe him, because he's right.

I have a good face. Great face, even. Maybe I'm a face actress more than a body actress. And you know what else? It's cool that everyone in my family had something to do with the movie. It makes us one of those showbiz families.

Just like the ones you read about in *People*.

MY FAMILY IS A SHOWBIZ FAMILY.

12 YEARS
5 MONTHS
24 DAYS

Dear Actors and Actresses,

I'm so sorry for the delay in announcing the cast for <u>Welcome to the Circus Hotel, Hollywood DiVecchio!</u>

I know it's been a long wait for a lot of you. Unfortunately, I had a little unexpected drama of my own and wasn't able to be here. But I'm happy to say that I am back at school now and will be announcing the cast tomorrow.

I'm looking forward to a great show and really appreciate your talent and your patience.

Sincerely,
Mrs. Belter

12 YEARS
5 MONTHS
25 DAYS

This is how it went today after school:

FAIRMOUNT ELEMENTARY SCHOOL DRAMA CLUB
ANNOUNCES THE CAST FOR THE WINTER PLAY

WELCOME TO THE CIRCUS HOTEL,
HOLLYWOOD DiVECCHIO!
Adapted by Howard Dewin

Big thanks to all the amazing student actors who came out to audition. You were *all* amazing! If you don't see your name here, it just means that this time, for these particular roles, with these actors, this was the best arrangement . . . in my opinion. At another time, with different people, it could just as easily be a whole different group of actors. Please think about lending your talents to the show in other ways this year. It takes a lot more than actors to make a great play! As for the actors who *do* see their names listed below—congratulations! Please see me to pick up your scripts and rehearsal schedule.

Hollywood	Heidi Stewart
Hollywood's Mom	Tessa Fountain
Grandfather	Mr. C.
Nel the Fat Lady	Lainey McBride
Timbo the Strong Man	Jim Manikowski
Twins Gymnastica	Michaela Bradshaw & Susan Sanchez
Jack the Lion Trainer	Don Baudine
Olga the Wee Lion	Cindy Bennett
Chewy	Diane Tewksbury
Rodnifico	Steve Massie

I'm just standing outside the music room staring at the announcement.

Lenore and Tammy are standing right behind me, but I think they're afraid to say anything. Plus, Lenore must have known I was going to get this part and so she must be feeling really guilty at this point. At least, she better be feeling guilty!

Seriously? The Fat Lady? How could Mrs. Belter do this to me? I'm going to turn down the role. That's all there is to it. There is no way I am going to stand up on a stage and talk about how fat I am!

"Lainey?"

I spin around. Mrs. Belter is standing in her open doorway. "May I speak with you privately for a minute?"

I want to yell at her, tell her she is being really mean! But she always looks so nice when she smiles that it's impossible to do anything but smile back and do whatever she asks.

Tammy and Lenore clear out of my way so I can walk into the music room. Mrs. Belter shuts the door, but I can see Tammy and Lenore standing frozen in the middle of the hallway watching us through the long, skinny piece of glass in the door.

"Here is your script, Lainey. It's a very big part. You will have a lot on your shoulders with this play. Your character is really the driving force—if the audience doesn't root for her, they will never root for Hollywood to find a way to stay and live the life of the circus. And we need the audience to do that or the play won't work."

I mean to open my mouth so I can tell her that I'm not taking the part, but instead, my head nods. I cannot say I had actually realized Nel was that important. Still, it doesn't really seem to make a difference with the pit in my stomach.

Because honestly? All I can see is that Nel's FAT.

Mrs. Belter is quiet for a minute and then she says, "I know you wanted Hollywood, Lainey. But I will tell you something if I can have your word that it stays between us."

It takes me a minute to nod just because I don't think I've ever been told a secret by a teacher. It takes a little extra processing.

"Hollywood is a young girl about your age with a lot of the same feelings and thoughts that girls your age have. It's a simpler role to play. Nel is more complicated. I need a real actress to play her."

I'm trying to let the words sink in because I know what she's saying is more important than the fact that the character is fat, but it's really hard to get past it. I might have been a little more successful if I didn't, at that same moment, see a fat suit hanging up in the corner of the room.

"I saw a fat suit just like that at The Play's the Thing," I say.

"That *is* the fat suit from The Play's the Thing. Mr. Mankewicz is my uncle. He's very good about helping me with the school play."

"He's your uncle?" I repeat.

Mrs. Belter smiles one of those smiles and nods.

"But why do you need a fat suit?" I ask her.

She looks surprised for a second and then she says "It's for you, Lainey. For you to use when you play Nel."

"Me?"

Suddenly, Mrs. Belter laughs. Then she says, "Lainey, YOU are not the Fat Lady. You are PLAYING the Fat Lady. That's why you got this role and nobody else. I need someone who understands the difference between saying lines and playing a role, who has the talent to find the heart and soul of someone who is not at all like her, and who has enough confidence and bravery to show that person to the world even if it's not exactly the way the actress would like to be seen herself."

It's hard to describe what's happening because it is totally going on inside me. Something is cracking wide open. Mrs. Belter's words are bouncing around inside my head. I feel really calm even though I'm totally excited. And the words in my head are starting to form sentences in my heart and then those sentences are turning into paragraphs in my bones. It's so weird.

It's not like I understand in my head what she just said. It's more like, I feel what she just said—in my body and soul.

That's when something moves by the door and catches my eye. Tammy and Lenore aren't standing in the middle of the hallway anymore. They are right up against the door. Their worried faces are filling that skinny pane of glass. I've got to tell you, right now they look pretty silly and they look pretty great—like the best friends ever.

I swear a big window is opening up inside me and a lot more light is shining through. It makes it much easier to see what's important and what's not.

For those working on my biography, this is where you might say, "For Lainey McBride, things were starting to look up."

DEAR DUMB DIARY,

CHECK OUT JAMIE KELLY'S DEAR DUMB DIARY BOOKS!

YEAR TWO:
#1: School. Hasn't This Gone
On Long Enough?

YEAR TWO:
#2: The Super-Nice are
Super-Annoying

#1: Let's Pretend This Never Happened

#2: My Pants Are Haunted!

#3: Am I the Princess or the Frog?

#4: Never Do Anything, Ever

#5: Can Adults Become Human?

#6: The Problem With Here Is That It's Where I'm From

#7: Never Underestimate Your Dumbness

#8: It's Not My Fault I Know Everything

#9: That's What Friends <u>Aren't</u> For

#10: The Worst Things In Life Are Also Free

#11: Okay, So Maybe I Do Have Superpowers

#12: Me! (Just Like You, Only Better)

Our Dumb Diary: A Journal to Share

Totally Not Boring School Planner